Until the colours sing

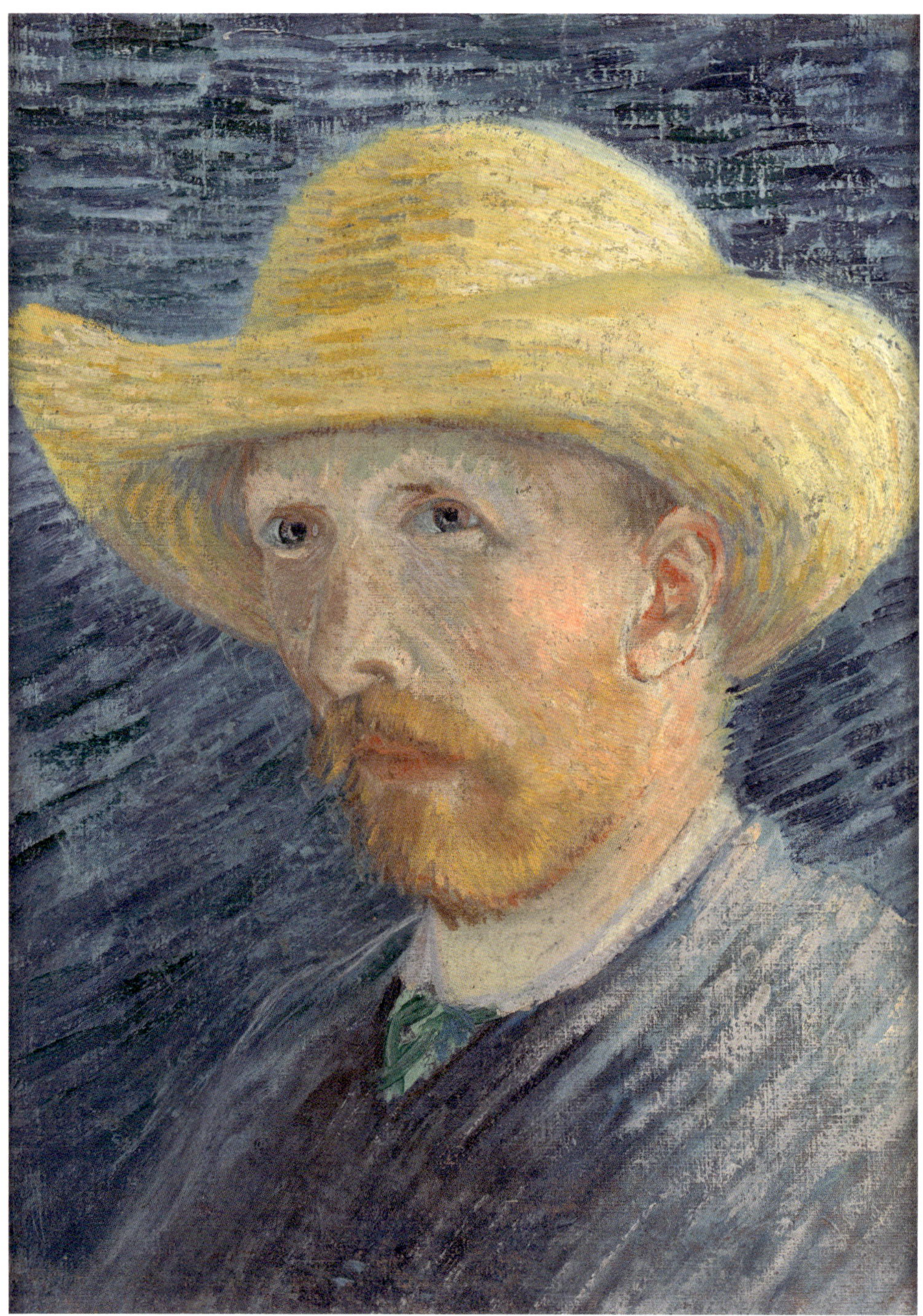

Self-Portrait with Straw Hat 1887

Until the colours sing

Paul de Moor

snoeck

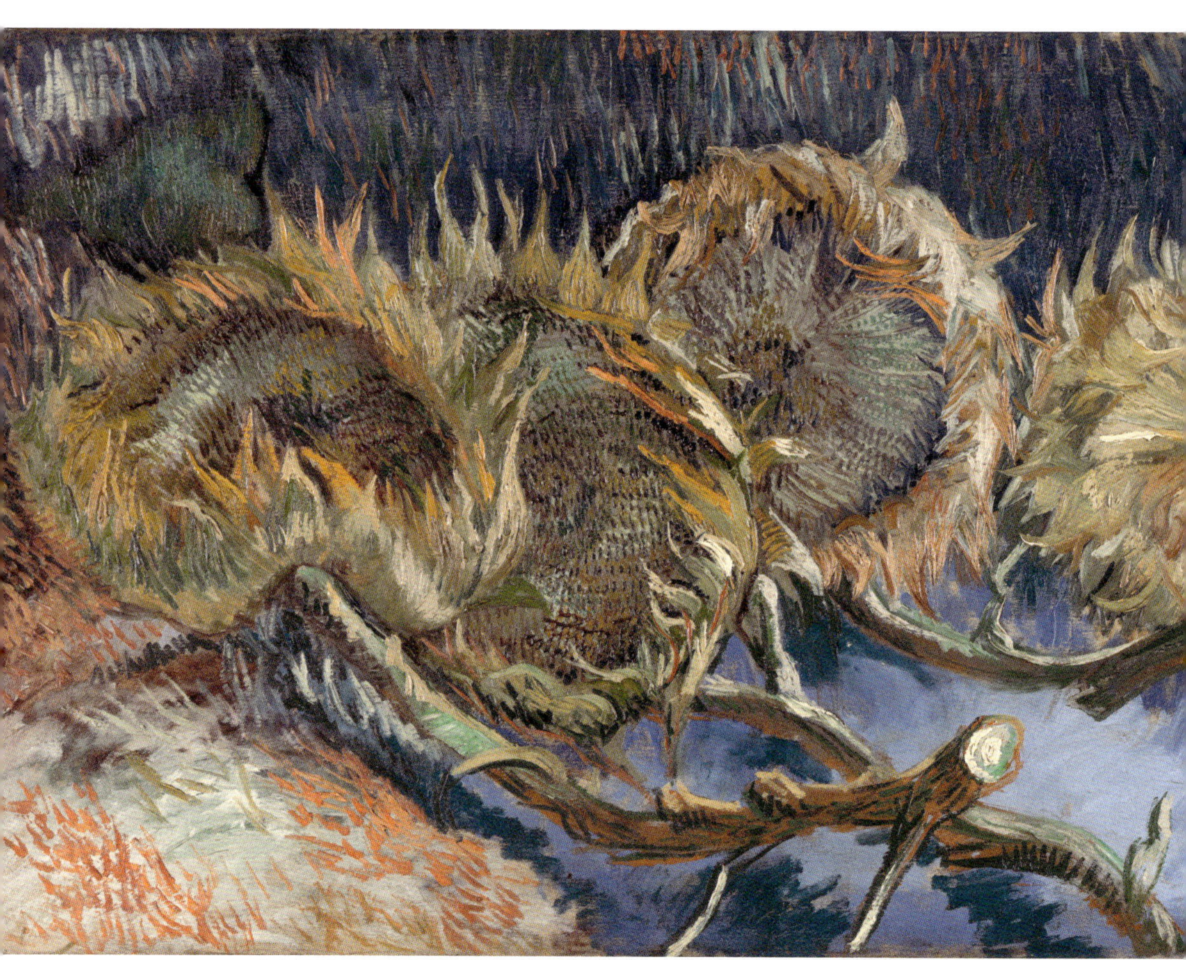

Four Sunflowers Gone to Seed 1887

« 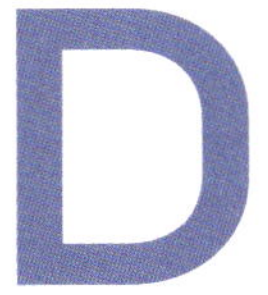o what sunflowers do, » says father.
« Look into the sun. Bloom yellow-coloured, » says mother.
« Just do it, » says father.
« Become a boy with spirit, » says mother.
« I'll draw, » Little Sunflower insists. « And paint. I'll paint everything I see and hear and smell. I'll paint us, the sunflowers. And those folks over there, fishing potatoes out of the bowl. And the burning of the sun I'll paint. The tossing of the moon. The dancing of the stars in the sky. The howling of red in the trees. The blue hills. The yellow houses.
The golden fields and the wooden bridges over the ditches.
Everything I see that you don't see. I'll paint in a million colours, » says little Sunflower.
« In a million colours, » says father.
« The howling of red in the trees, » says mother.
« The dancing of the stars in the sky, » says father.
« See? » says little Sunflower. « I see what you don't see. »
« Just stand in my shadow, » says father.
« I'll move up a bit, » says sister.
« Boy, » says mother.
« I'll take you at your word, » says brother.

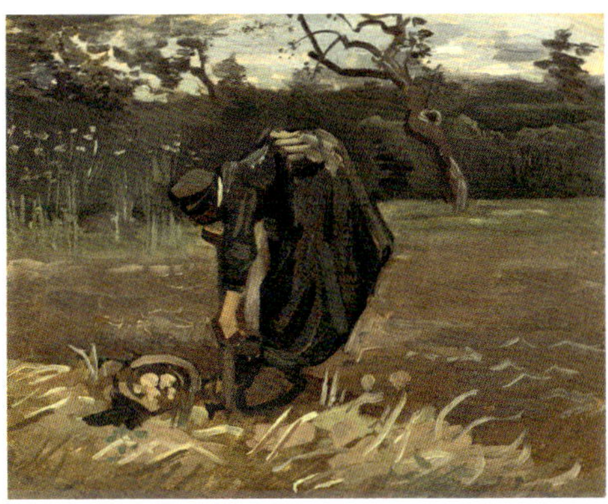

Peasant Woman Digging Potatoes 1885

« **Are you really going to be a painter?** »

asks brother.

« **I'm colour** »,

says little Sunflower.

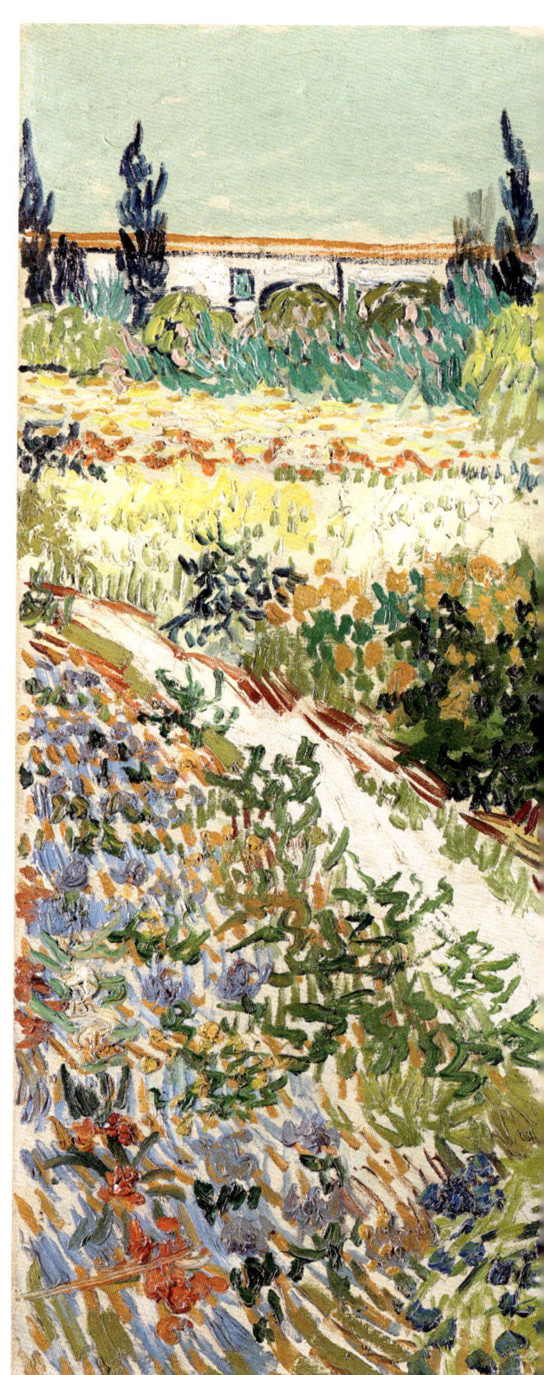

Garden at Arles 1888

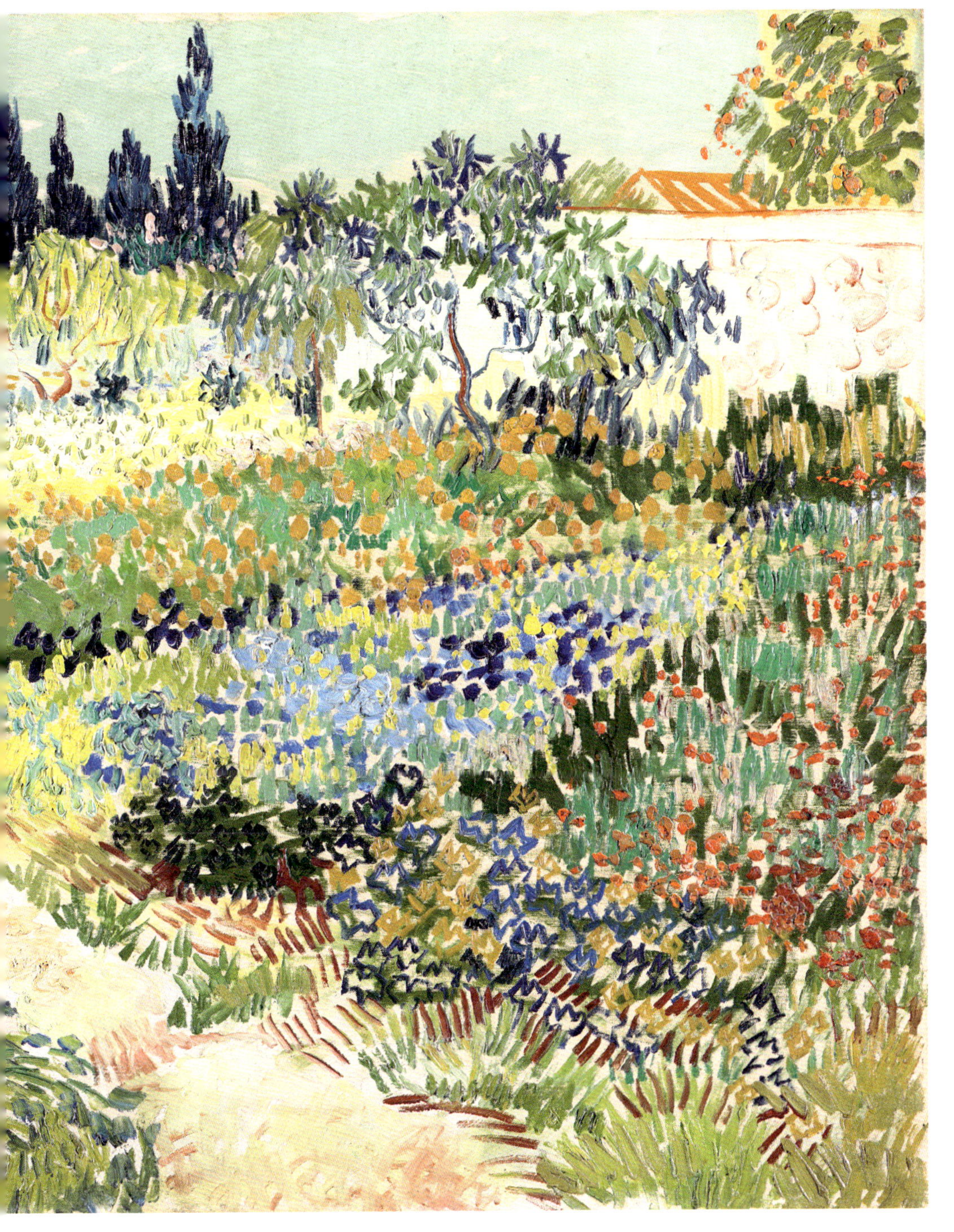

Little Sunflower tells his brother his secrets, whispering them into his left ear. How many yellows he will paint. The harsh yellow of the sun. The golden yellow of the wheat and the red yellow in the flowerbed. Not forgetting the lemon yellow in the arms of the chair.

« I'll brush the blue of the clouds over the fields, » he says.
« And the purple of evening over the blue of morning. I'll capture the blood-red of the setting sun in the soft pink of the candlelight. »

« And what about the greens? » asks brother.
« The greens, » says little Sunflower. « There are so many greens. There's the white green of the dew. The black green on the oak table-top. The orange green in the trees. The purple green of the leaves. »

« And I'll paint all the blacks, brother. »
« All the blacks? »
« The yellow black. The white black. The black black. The sunny black. The sad black. The vibrant black. The striped black. The flat black. The black in the light. »
« The black in the light? »
« Just look, brother. Look into the light. »

« And I'll paint all the whites, brother. »
« All the whites? »
« Don't you see them? All those whites? The grey white. The yellow white. The black white. The red white. The shadow white? The blue white of the snow and the blue under the ice? »

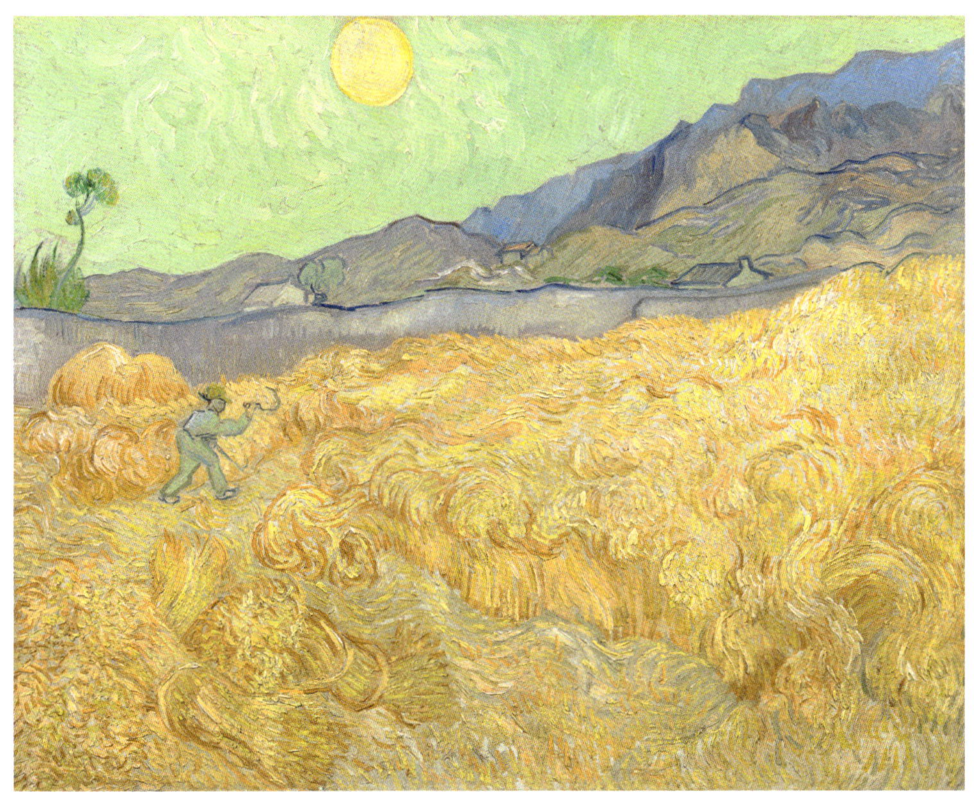

Wheatfield with a Reaper 1889

« The colours are
bursting out of my head,
brother.
I can't wait. »

« Can't you two
ever
be quiet », asks father.

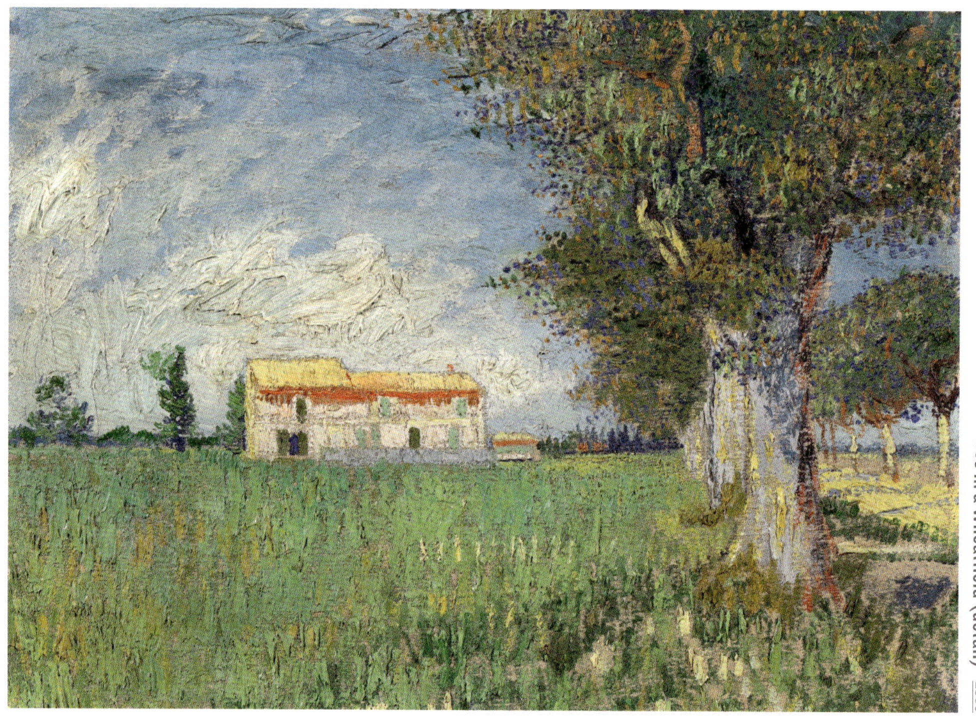

Farmhouse in a Wheatfield (detail) 1888

«

I can't stop looking at the clouds, brother. I see the sun up in the clouds. She outlines them in gold. And if not a golden rim, then a silver rim. The clouds are constantly turning into statues. Into thunderstorm towers. Into heads and faces, into sheep, into reptiles. They rush in, shaking and upturning entire landscapes. I paint the joy of the clouds and the anger of the clouds. For it's the sun that shows me the clouds, brother. That conjures up the purple clouds in the green sky. What might it be like up there? Above the clouds? Does anyone know? And from the clouds I look down at the landscapes. The sun's paths lead me there. And I paint. In the scorched land I paint the scent of wild thyme. I use mud to paint the brown purple in the potato skins. With the same mud I paint the bluish purple in the potato noses and on the potato faces. I paint hands of copper earth. Feet as clumps of willows. Eyes of turbid water. With the depth of green-coloured confusion. Or the violet of laughter and the wine-red of sadness. My brushes shoot in all directions. Left to right, top to bottom, horizontally, dripping like rain. In wavy lines. In short stripes. With my thumb, with my fingers. With the tips of my brushes. To paint all that, I have to move fast, brother. Fast to look, to see, to smell, be free. Running hither and thither. And further. And always further. To the edge. Till over the edge. Yes, even till over the edge.

»

The Ravin (Les Peiroulets) 1889

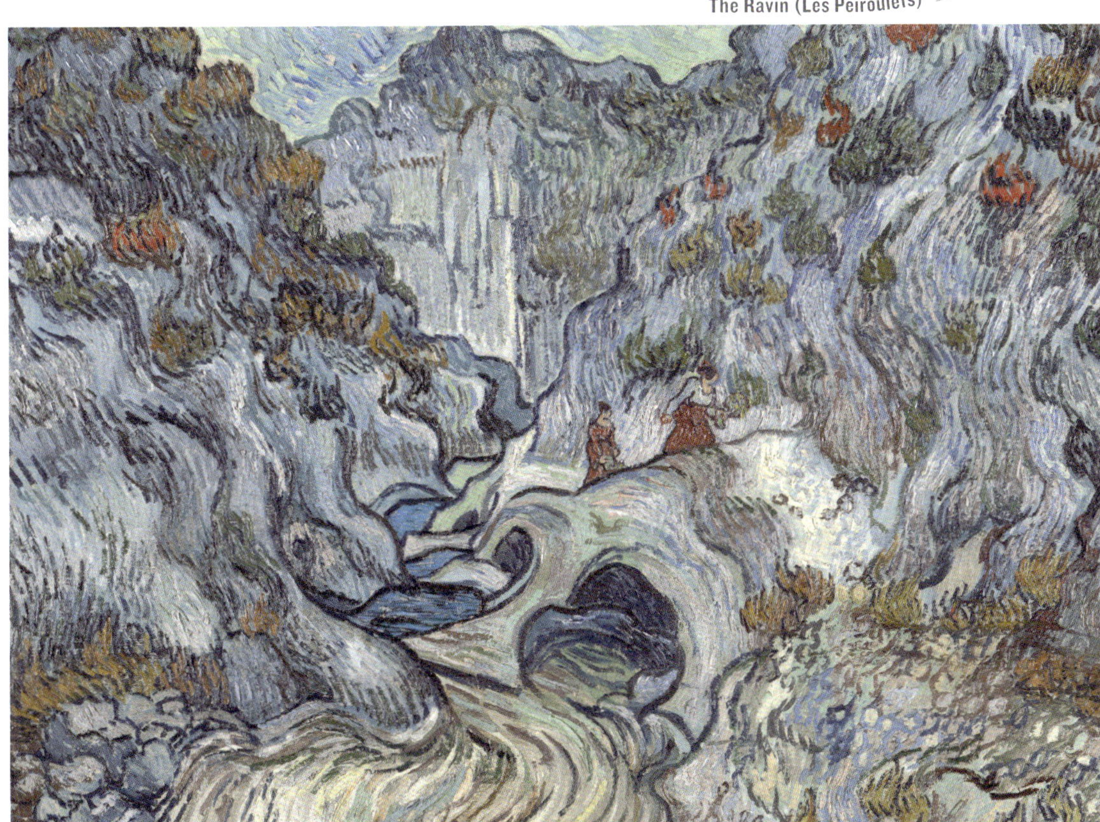

«

I am in the south, brother. Deep in France. The light down here is powerful. The shadows are boiling white. The bright red of the afternoon dissolves into the baked earth. The early evening fades the simple blue to violet. The nocturnal yellow dissolves into orange patches. And there are the sounds, brother. The buzzing of the bees in the lavender fields. The chirping of the crickets in the olive trees. The croaking of the jays. It goes so far that the stars keep me awake with their white twinkling. I've no time to waste, brother. I have to get a move on. The moon turns yellow round and round in my head. She demands I paint her, over and over again. Today I paint the red landscapes with the green and blue hills. The trees with the red trunks in the lemon-yellow sky. The sun shines here for painters. My paint is my food. My work is my drink. My canvases are my bed. Yesterday I painted sunflowers from early morning till late evening. In the sunflowers I painted father, mother, you, myself. I'm a sunflower myself. I painted the sunflowers from the field and the sunflowers in the jar. Sunflowers become only more beautiful when looked at for a long time. How I long for you, brother. A fierce desire I also paint into the sunflowers. Life radiates from the burnt yellow. Death lurks in the black heart. Sunflowers are special, brother. We're special, brother. In no other flower are life and death so closely intertwined. And they die standing, sunflowers. As we shall die standing. When I have more canvases ready I'll send them to you. It's hard work. It may take a while. Sunflowers cannot simply be captured in a few strokes of paint. They also want to be real on canvas. No. They want to be real, especially on canvas. Whether they beam with joy. Or bow withered heads.

»

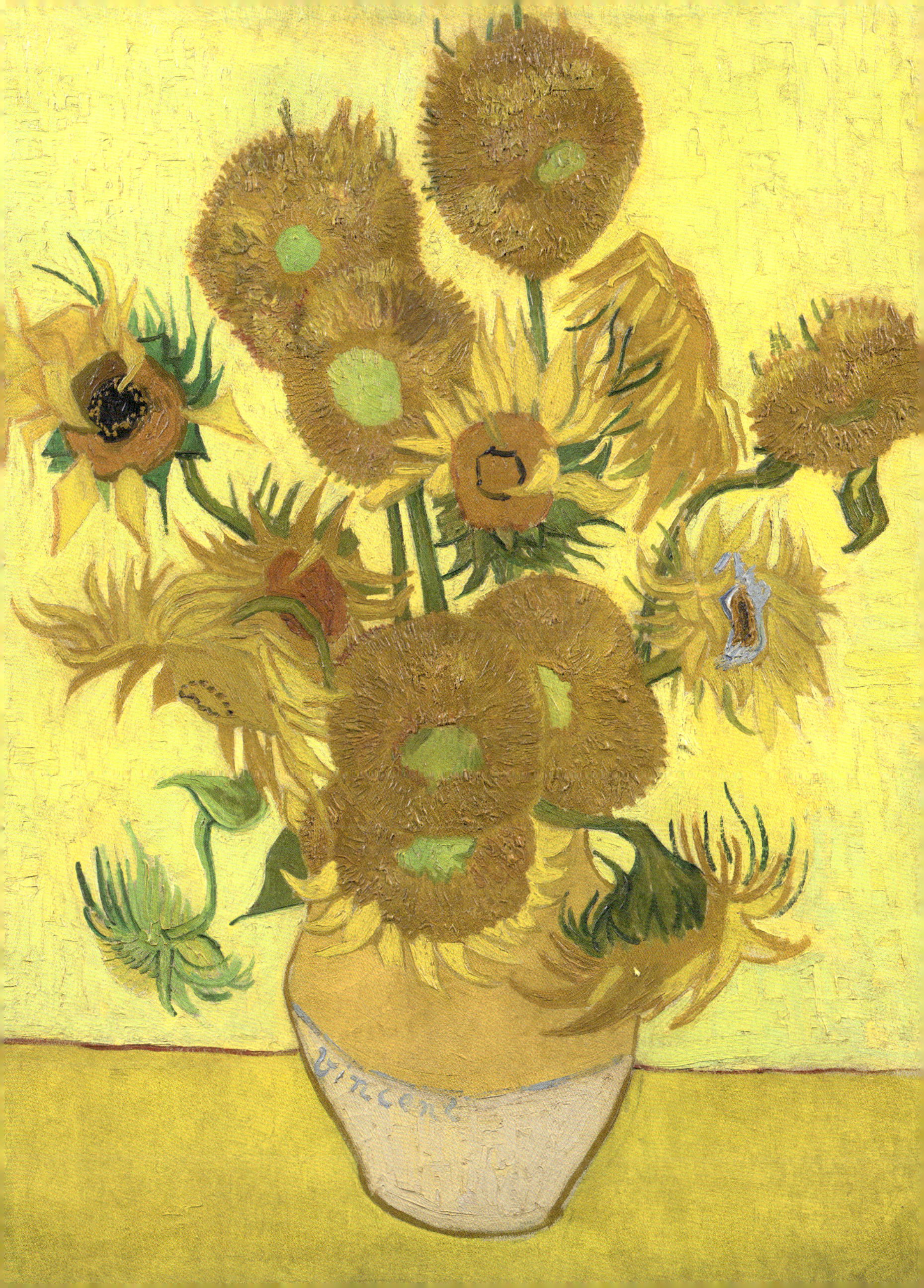
Vincent

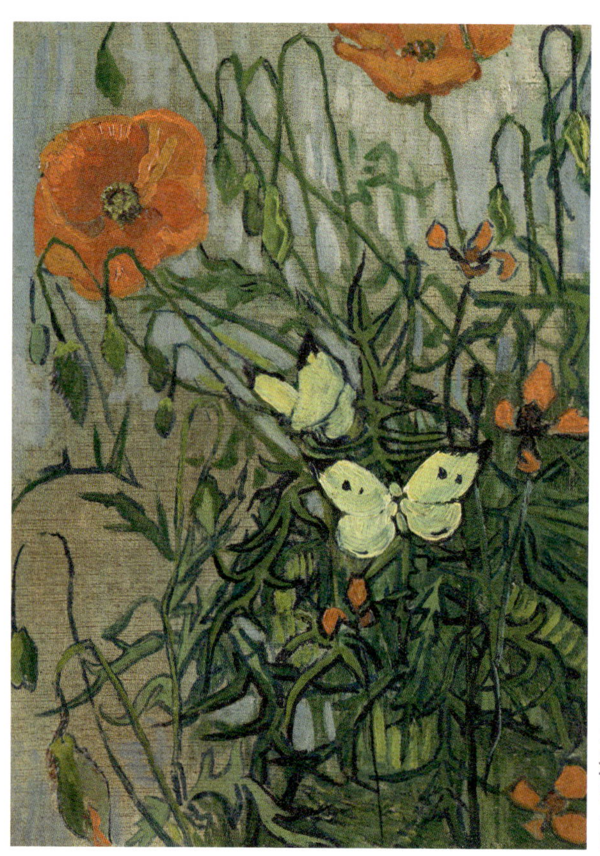

Butterflies and Poppies 1889

« Hello brother. Today I'm painting portraits from memory and I'm painting the way people in Japan live like flowers. »

«

I am in a hurry, brother. This morning I took my easel to a deserted spot. Far from the village. To a piece of land where the wind and clouds have free rein. To play? Yes, brother, to play. The sun, the clouds, the wind, it's a game without beginning or end. The sun on the clouds, the wind in the clouds and the rushing clouds that the sunlight on the fields chases away with their shadows. It's a game I can watch for hours. A game that makes me reach for my paint box. I had to use rope to tie the legs of my easel to iron pegs. The wind was crazy. It came rolling out of the hills. Picked up speed. Somersaulted. Became a storm, ripping my clothes off. If I hadn't tied down my easel, the wind would have blown it across the river and over the distant hills. You should have seen the colours rushing past. Flying in all directions. Like startled chickens running from a fox. They shot from left to right, bumping against each other. I heard them cackling, the colours. The dust made the green dirty and the yellow opaque. I caught as much colour as I could. With whole slabs of paint. With fat streaks. With thin streaks. With choppy strokes. With whorls. With throwing and flinging. It was quite a challenge, capturing the roar of the wind on the canvas. The roaring also in my head. I don't know if I succeeded. On my canvas the wind tears the sun to shreds. It pulls the olive trees crooked. Hills bend their tops. It sweeps branches back and forth. Roots seek a foothold in the stony earth and curl hands and fingers together as if in prayer. Birds swoop black through the air. That's how I saw it, brother. That's how it was. That's how I painted it. With all its vehemence. In haste. In the chase. Breathless. I'm a wild hunter, brother. Are you listening to my canvases?

»

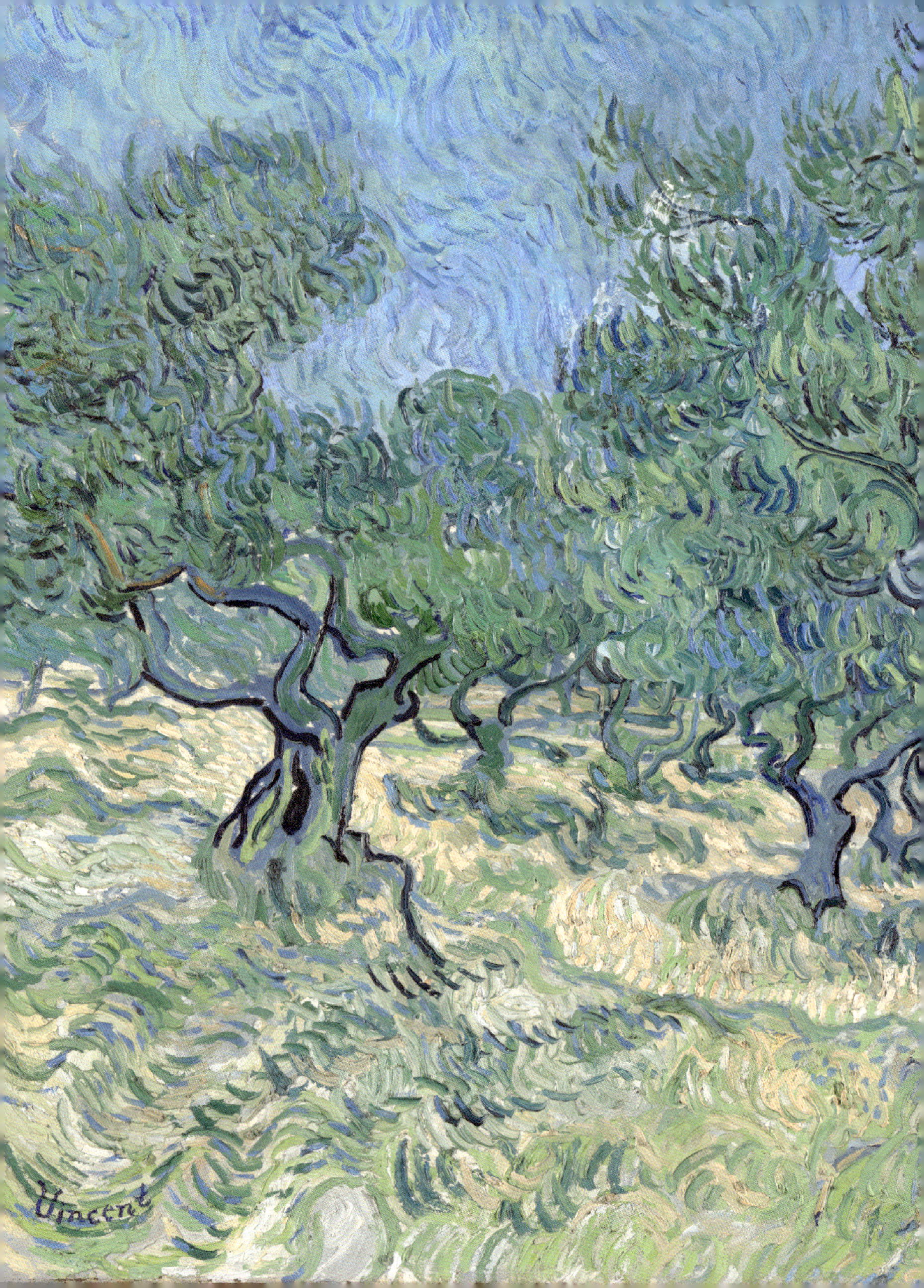
Vincent

« Hello brother. I am lonely and poor. I'm a broken jar, but the more I'm a broken jar, the more I become an artist. »

Still Life with Jars 1885

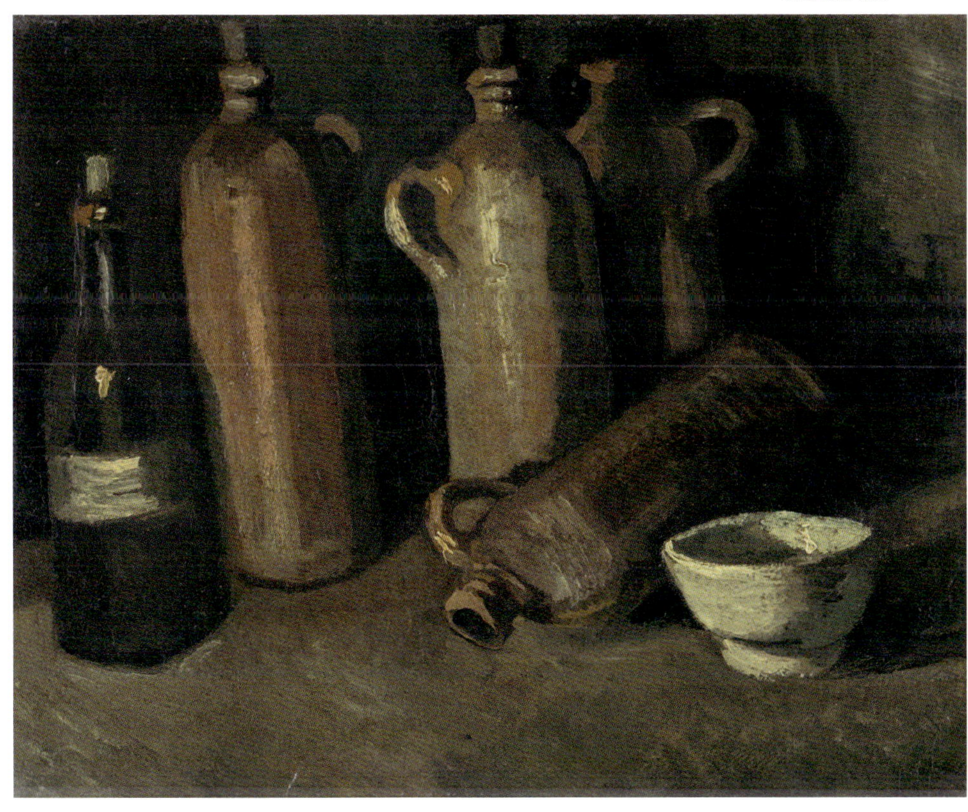

Olive Grove **(detail)** 1889

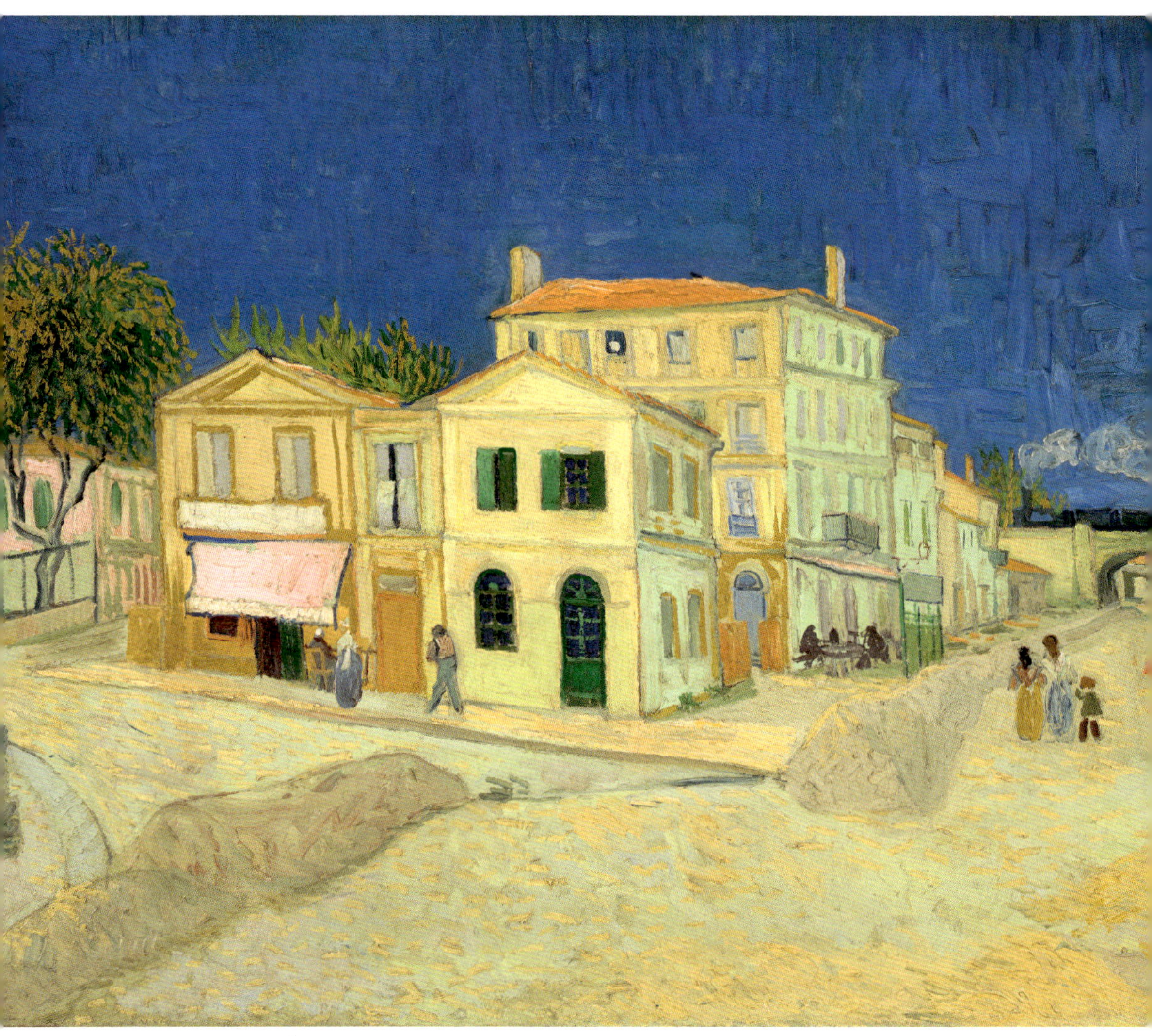

The Yellow House (The Street) 1888

«

I am painting my yellow house, brother. I paint it at all hours of the day. I can't get enough of it. The house spurs me on. It forces me. It lures me and won't let me go. And I'm picking up the gauntlet. Early in the morning. Late at night. Often in the afternoon. When the sun scorches the earth. When the sun bends straight lines. When the crickets sing hoarsely. When the green shutters of my yellow house turn almost black. It's terribly hot in the full sun, brother. So hot that I'm in danger of flaking out. This afternoon, blue and red flames danced on my straw hat. To capture the scene, I squeezed the hottest yellow from my tubes. A yellow that sets house and canvas on fire. A yellow that burns my eyes. But when I got to that point, I plucked fresh, bright blues from the sky. I extinguished the hardest yellow with the softest blue. With a crooked tree I brought in some shade. Colours reinforce each other, brother. Or extinguish each other. Don't red and blue make purple? And yellow and red make orange? And blue and yellow make green? If I paint red and yellow and blue one after another I see a patch of black. But in and on the black there is movement, there has to be movement, because of the colours under it. A colour is a colour only if there is colour underneath it. Did I tell you that I put chairs with wicker seats in my yellow house? That I decorated the walls with my sunflowers? I think of you, of all of you. Sunflowers are everywhere here, brother, wherever I look. They're beautiful, even withered. I'm one myself, aren't I?

»

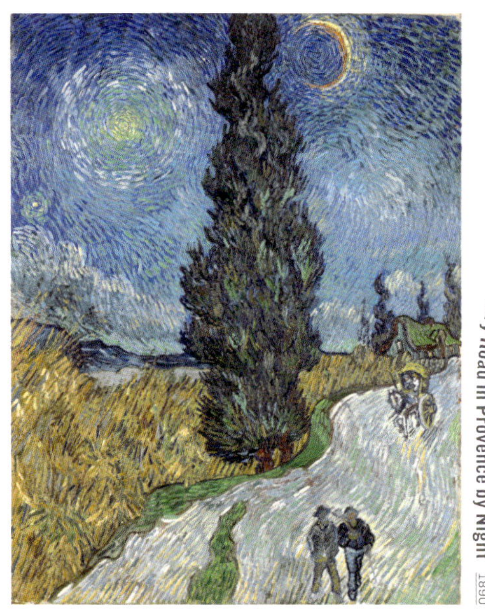

Country Road in Provence by Night 1890

«I paint like crazy, brother, until the brush falls from my hands.»

«My head's spinning, brother. Like it spins in the starry sky. I lay on my back in the grass in the garden. Under the almond tree. The grass was hard and dry. It cracked like snow. The sun shone blithely. A grasshopper made a strange jump, from my stomach onto my straw hat. I left the earth. My body rose. Hesitantly at first. But then faster and faster. It turned on its axis. I closed my eyes and opened them again. I was floating among the white blossoms in the branches. Sailing through the many blues in the sky. The birds were slippery fish. That one cloud on the horizon was a ship's sail. It was silent. Lost in a motionless sea. And then, then, a bird hopped up onto my chest. On both legs at once. I jumped up. I had to paint what I saw, paint what was happening inside me. The snow white of the blossoms. The greys and greens in the tree's branches. The swirling blues in the air. The vibrating colours in my head.

I painted with bated breath, brother. The restlessness inside me mixed with the paint on the canvas. I painted until my painting was good. Until I found the silence of the white. But it's never good, brother. It's never good enough. I'm always wanting to paint what I see in another way. Always paint better. Always painting like a sunflower. I'll never find peace. Never. The bird on my chest settles down and then flies right back up. The spinning in my head will always be there. Always.

»

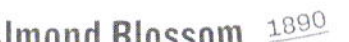

Almond Blossom 1890

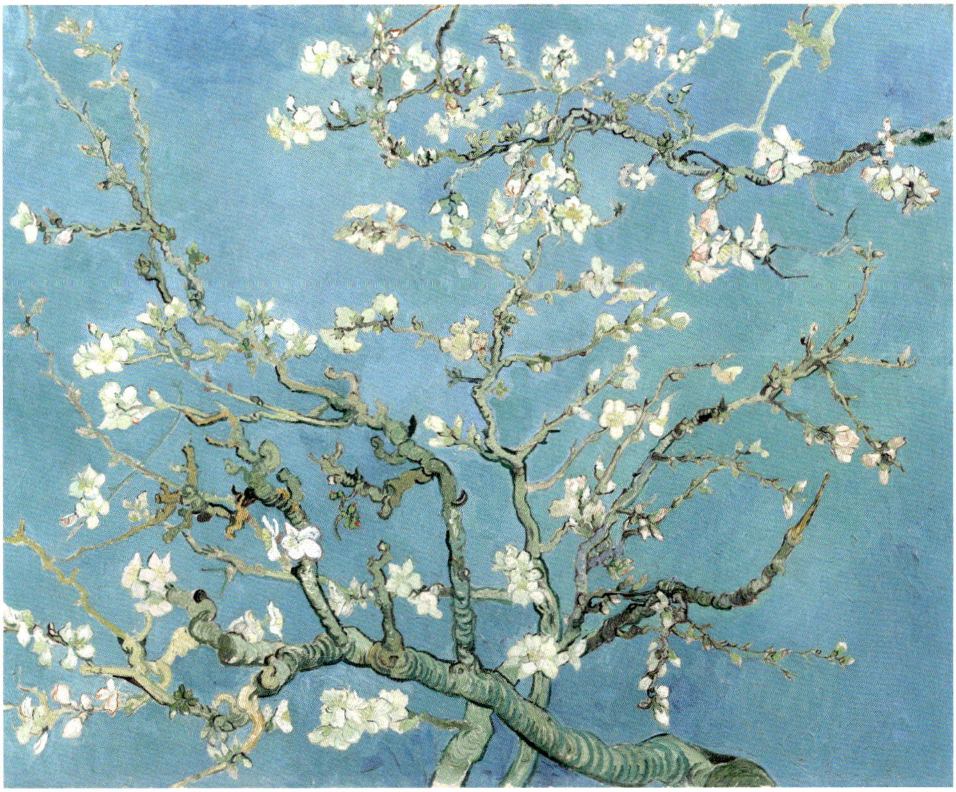

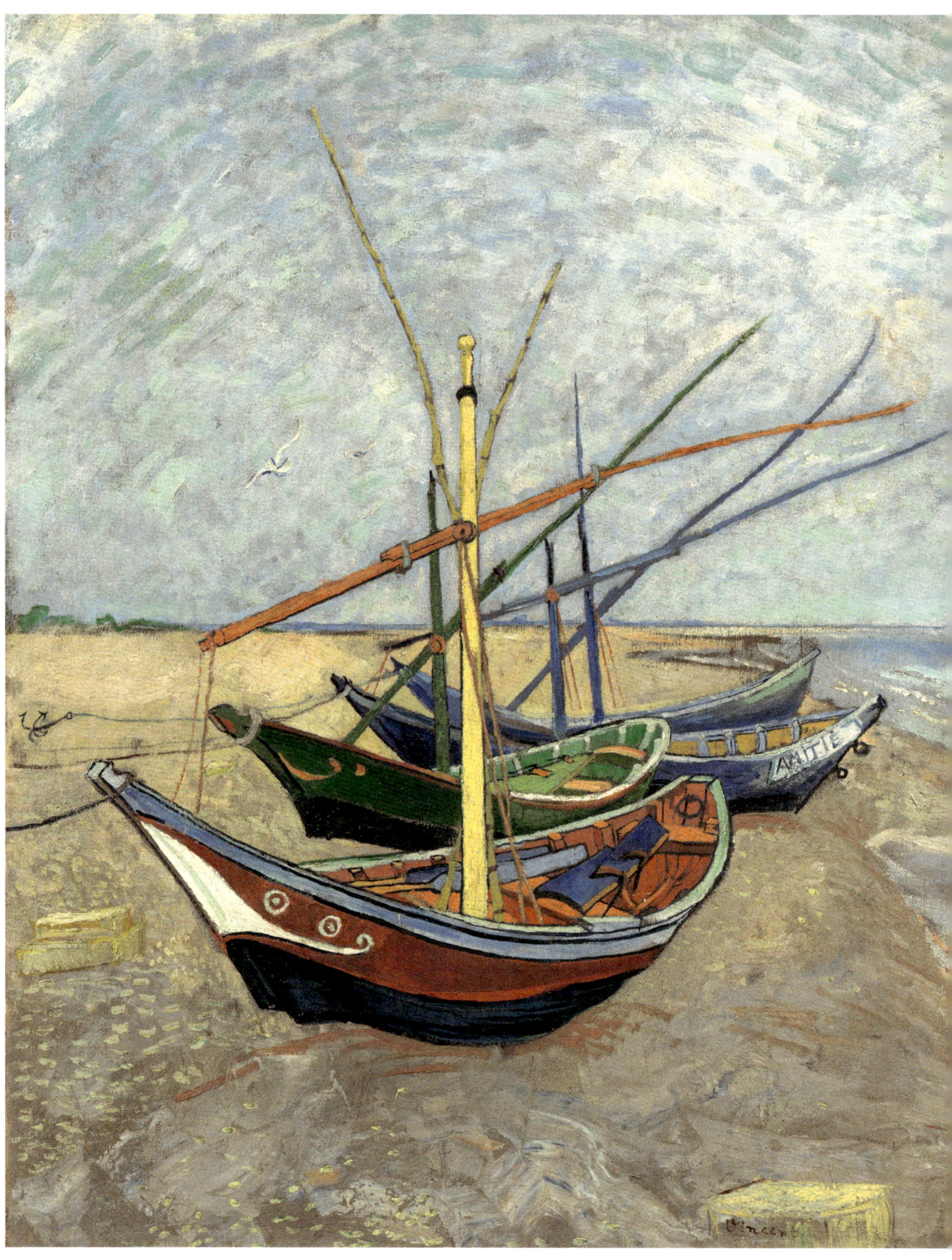
AMITIE

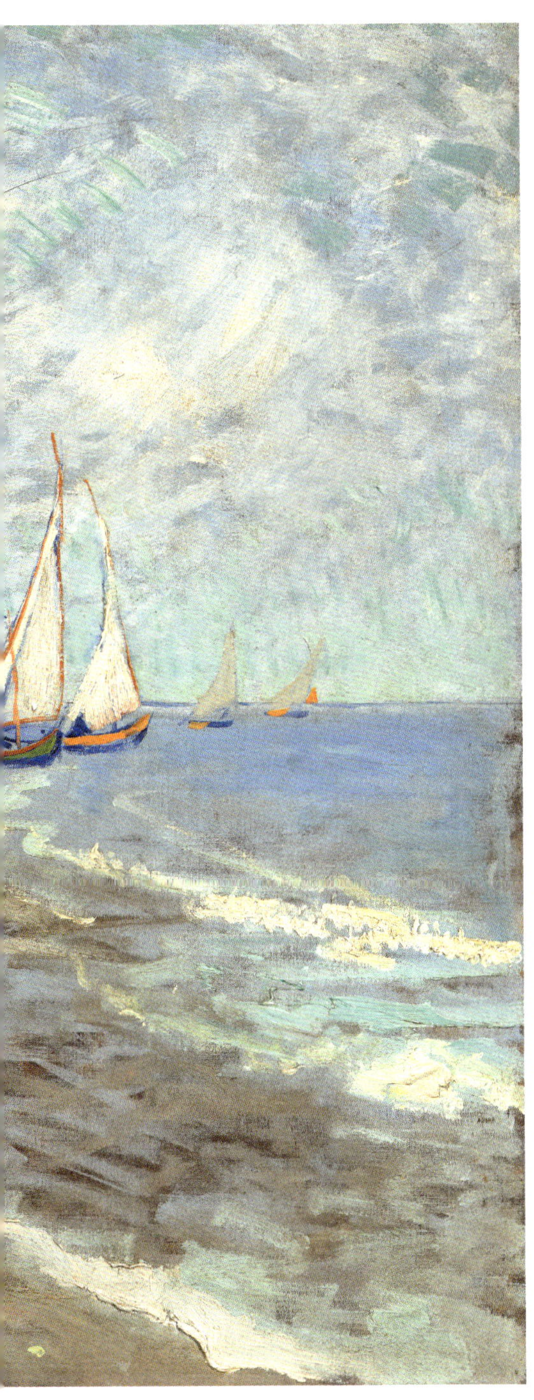

Fishing Boats on the Beach at Les Saintes-Maries-de-la-Mer 1888

« I always wear
a hat, brother.
A straw hat
in good weather,
a black hat
in rain and wind.
The sun is
blinding also
for sunflowers. »

«

don't sit still, brother. I've arrived, washed up at the sea's edge. After a long march. Through hill and valley. I slept in the open air. Ate next to nothing. Different places, different skies, colours, smells, sounds. The deep sighing of the sea excites me. I look at the horizon, where the sky descends into sea. Or where the sea flows over into sky. What is it, waiting beyond the horizon, brother? What is to be found there? What lies behind every blank canvas I want to paint? The sea's so wide, brother. So endlessly wide. It's overflowing with colour. It's never the same for a moment. While I was painting it yesterday, it moved erratically like the wind and took on different shades. From blues to greens to greys to blacks to whites. I waited eagerly for the fishermen to return. With my painting equipment at the ready. The beach too was a sea. Waves of sand ran over it. In the sun the beach was golden. Under dark clouds it was made of mud. I painted the sloops coming ashore and the fishing boats arriving. The sails were silver-grey white. The little boats in the distance weren't quite real, like dreams in search of a harbour. Or fits of dizziness in a tangle of colours. The ships' masts stood out yellow and blue against the sea and sky. One was wine-red. For the fishermen's wives it was quite odd to find a sunflower on the beach. A sunflower with shaggy beard, red hair and faded straw hat. When night fell, I clambered up into the dunes. The clouds had golden sun-edges. The nail of the moon had been squeezed from a lemon peel. The hills were purple. The night was mauve, blue and green. A mantle littered with white specks that lit up and then went out. The next morning I looked intently at my seascapes. I saw I had painted the green, red and blue boats as flowers.

»

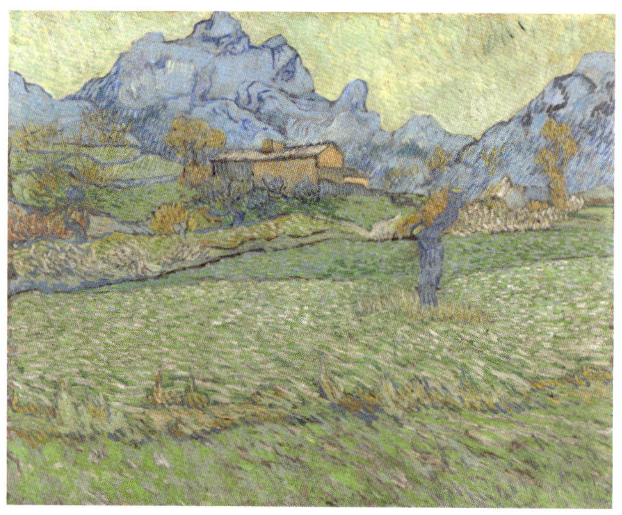

Wheatfields in a Mountainous Landscape *1889*

« I'm an explorer, brother. At times fearless, at times as timorous as a wet chicken. »

« I bathe here in the most sumptuous light, brother. Beautiful, radiant light even when the moon takes over the torch from the sun. Just imagine it. A faint source of light shrouds the moon in milky light. Wherever I look, stars light up. Clouds chase each other, tongues hanging out, grabbing and scrabbling for the stars, chasing the moon. They turn the night into a storm. Clouds are crazy dogs. It costs me blood, sweat and tears to capture on canvas their chasing and messing around. With all those blues and blacks, brother. With that white yellow and yellow white. At times I think there are more blues than stars in the universe. And nothing stands still. Everything moves. Everything rushes past. The colours move in waves and curls. They never stand still, brother. Nor do they on my canvases. They know neither rest nor stay. Each star rotates on its axis. The moon is a spinning top. I have too little paint to paint the colours of the night, brother. I really have to pull everything out of the box to paint the tossing and turning of the sky. With dots, streaks, strokes and violent sweeps of the brush. I rage like a devil. Jump back and forth. I paint with everything in me. My head and heart overflow with joy and anger. Joy in painting what I paint. Anger at trying to capture the impossible on canvas. I immerse the sky in blue green. I place the ground in mauve. The city in blue-yellow-black. I spread out the gaslight from the street lamps in yellow with red gold and streaks of dirty green. From the pebbles at the bottom of the river I make stars and gemstones. I dance around my canvases like a wild man, brother. The Big Bear reels around the Little One. The painter around the easel. Two people came to watch. They looked at my canvas and me. They didn't know what they were seeing.

»

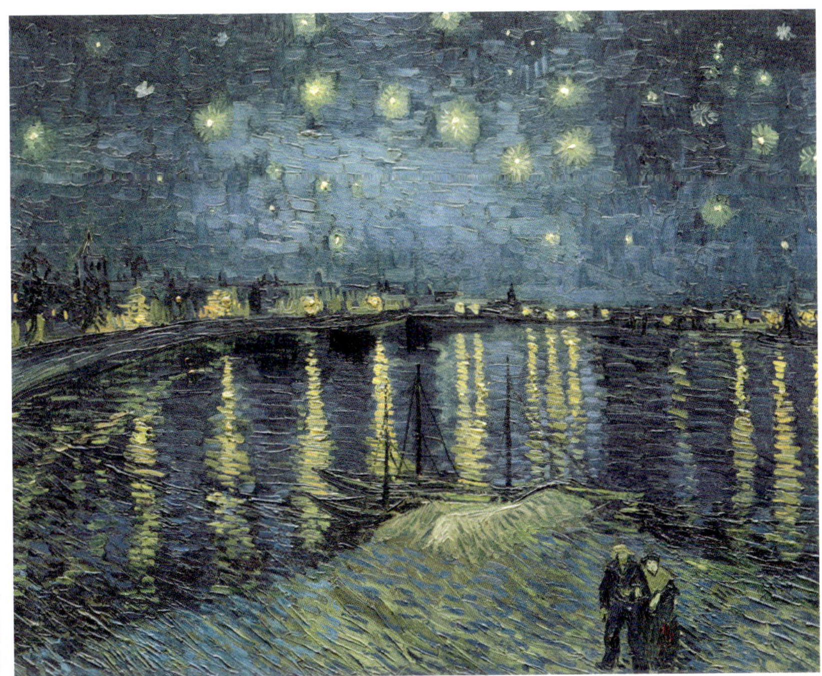

The Starry Night 1888

« **They laugh at**
me, brother.
They say I paint
the knight
with a wreath
of burning candles
on my
straw hat.
Let them do so.
They're crazy. »

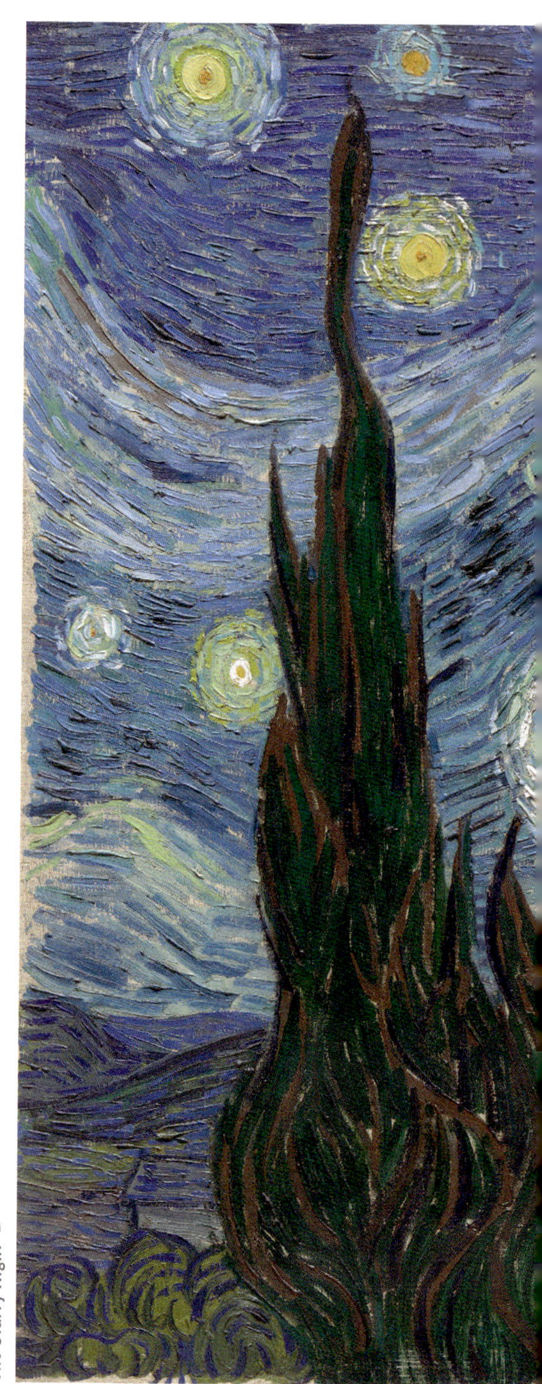

The Starry Night 1889

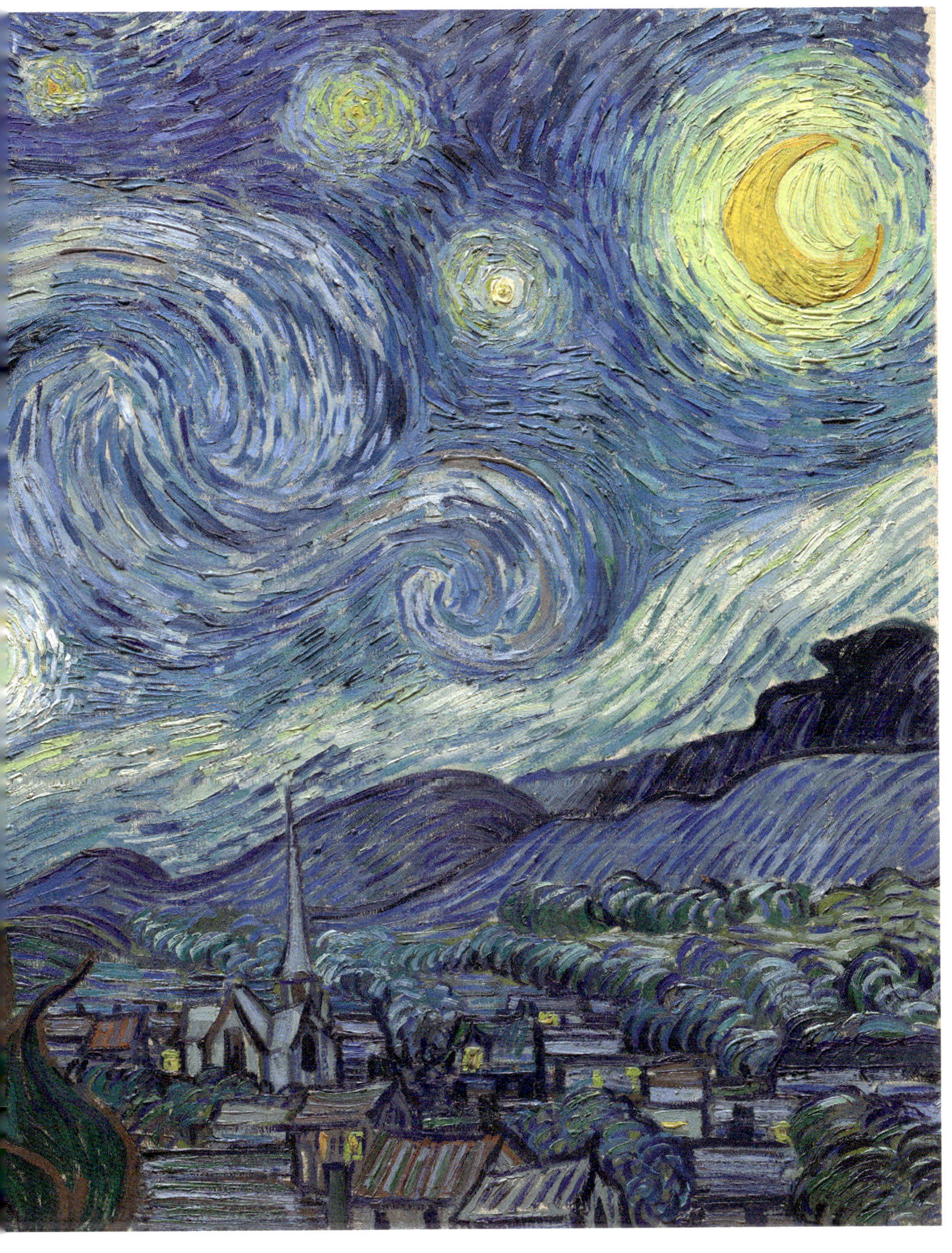

« I paint the people I know, brother. I paint them as friends. As passers-by. As fellow earth-dwellers. As potato eaters. And I paint the people I happen to cross along my way. The farmer in the field. The old person with closed eyes. The man with the grooves and cracks in his face. The old woman with a rope in her hands. The child. The men, women and children from the neighbourhood. I paint my doctor, that good man. I paint people like they painted saints of old. You know. Rembrandt, Vermeer, Hals and all those others who painted the saints in one way or another. Painted the saints as ordinary people. I want to breathe life into my portraits. Rich or poor. It doesn't matter. I want my portraits to feature real people. The grieving old man grieves, with my grief in his clenched fists. The people in the dance hall dance in a big movement. With my dance around the canvas. The poor creature is trapped in my poverty. I paint real people on real canvas in real colours, brother. I paint people who talk. Who tell stories. Who tell what they're doing. Or tell what they're not doing. Who keep silent and still tell. And I paint the books on the table. Also as friends. Because the books on the table are friends who never let me down. And I paint trees, brother. Lots of trees. Because trees are people. With crooked roots. With their heads in the clouds. With hanging arms. Or with arms raised. Just as chairs are people, brother. And the burning candle on the chair is a person. The candle keeps me company. It watches over me. At night, when

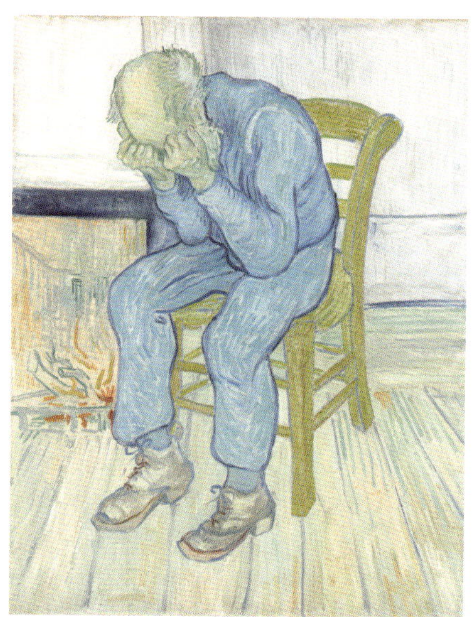

Sorrowing Old Man ('At Eternity's Gate') 1890

it's dark. During the day, when the sun fails to peek through the clouds. It wards off the evil spirits. It lights up my dreams. No matter how hard you blow, it won't go out.

»

« I walk in my worn shoes through the mud, brother, and I paint them. »

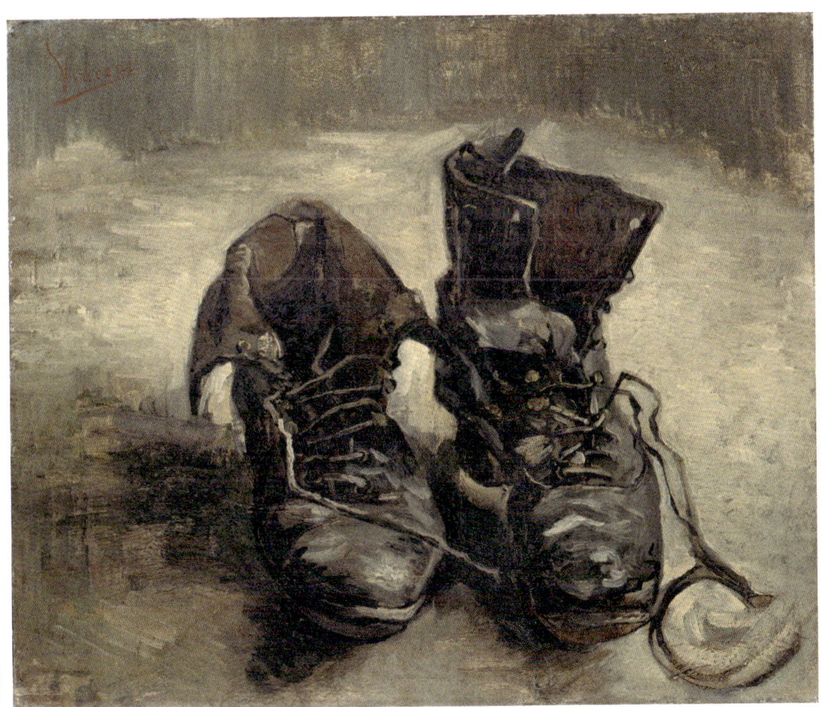

Shoes 1886

«

I paint the postman from down the street, brother. He carries out his work unfailingly. With the punctuality of a clock in the church tower. I could praise him to the heavens. He delivers your letters to me with care and helps me with posting my paintings. The other day I had him sit for me in his chair. He felt like a king. With his stiff postman's cap slightly crooked on his head. He's striking, brother. His face speaks. You don't immediately think of a postman when you see him. More like a gone-to-seed admiral of a sunken fleet. A hunk who has sailed the seven seas and weathered the most terrible storms. His nose disappears into his face. His shaggy moustache nibbles at his lips. His beard is a bush of wild growth. Doesn't he have the small grey eyes of a shrimp, our admiral? There are green, purple, pink and fiery shades in his bright red face. He removes his blue jacket with its gold buttons only to go to bed. Nor does he ever take off his cap. Not even to scratch his hair. There's beautiful gold stitching on his sleeves. He sat down in his customary manner. His right arm loosely over the chair arm. His left forearm at an angle on the corner of the table. His right hand extended, thumbs pointing away from his index fingers. There's as much colour in my postman as in his beard. Altogether the colours reveal a good person. Too old to be our father and yet our father. I'll ask him tomorrow to send his portrait to you. He's not at home right now. Perhaps he is on his rounds. I can't wait.

»

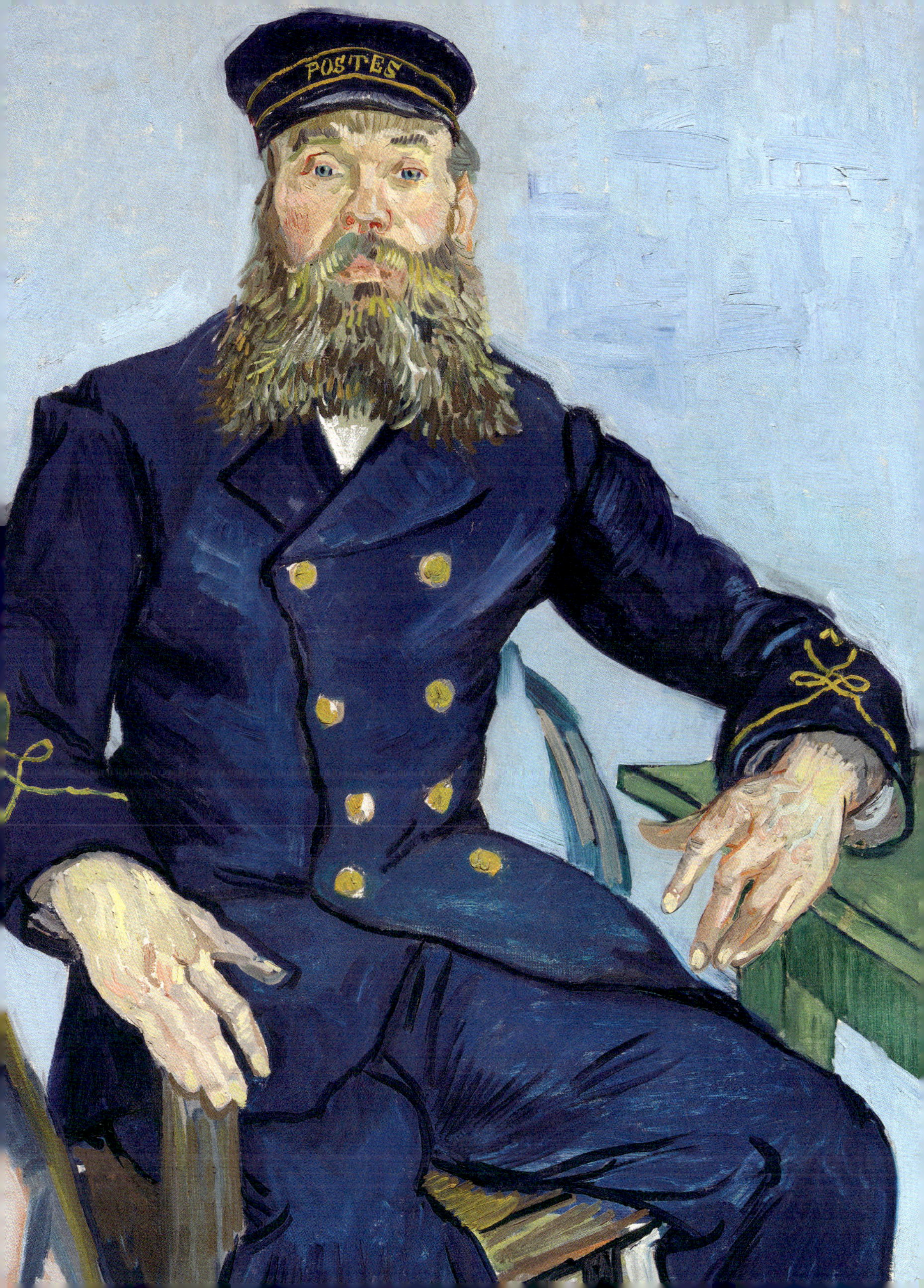
POSTES

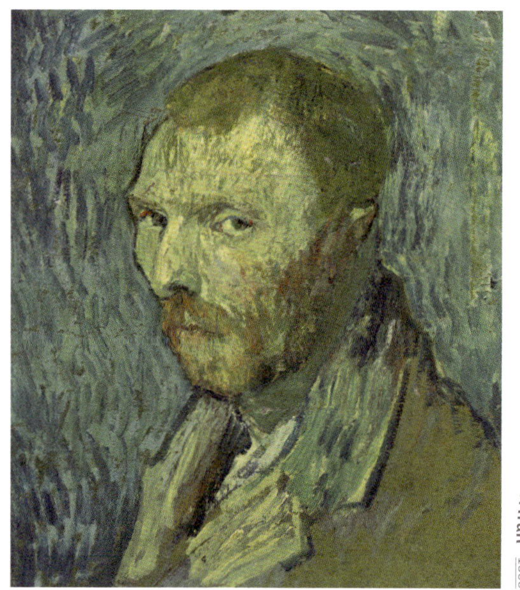

Self-Portrait 1889

« It's hell to paint myself, brother, that's why I paint myself as a thin, pallid devil. »

«

The twelve-year-old girl came my way unexpectedly, brother. She had something about her. Something that caught my eye. Something picturesque. Something not artificial. I asked if I could paint her. Yes, I could. It took me a week to get her portrait right. I painted her and overpainted her. I knew how to I had to do it, but my brush refused. The colours clashed. The paint wouldn't take. The canvas stretched against it. I couldn't find her face behind her face. I kept looking. Like the sun for the night. I lost my way. Tracked back the same way and got lost again. Until the image I was looking for fell into place and appeared in the correct colours. Until I found the right red and the right black to tie the red bow in her black hair. Until I found the right yellow. The yellow I needed to capture the pink and the pink yellow and the yellow pink of the matt tone of her face and hands. Until I found the right blood-red and orange gold for the blood-red dress. And I had the precious gold for the orange gold buttons. And the royal blue for the royal blue dress. How I searched for the orange and misty green for the orange dots against the misty green back wall. I pressed a bouquet of white flowers into her left hand. In this way I turned the girl into a flower in a bent chair. Flowers and I, brother, we're inseparable. And yes, chairs and me too. I could paint chairs every day. Chairs like sunflowers.

»

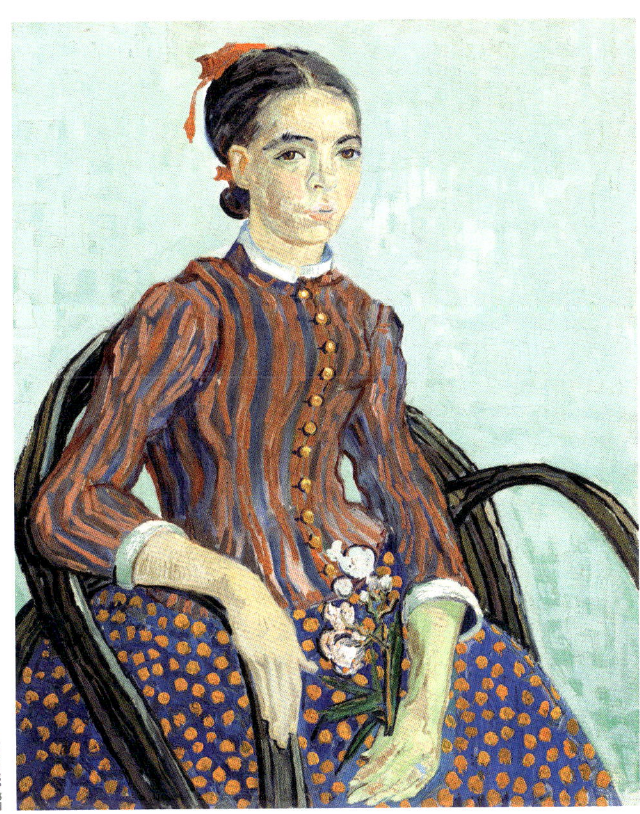

La Mousmé 1888

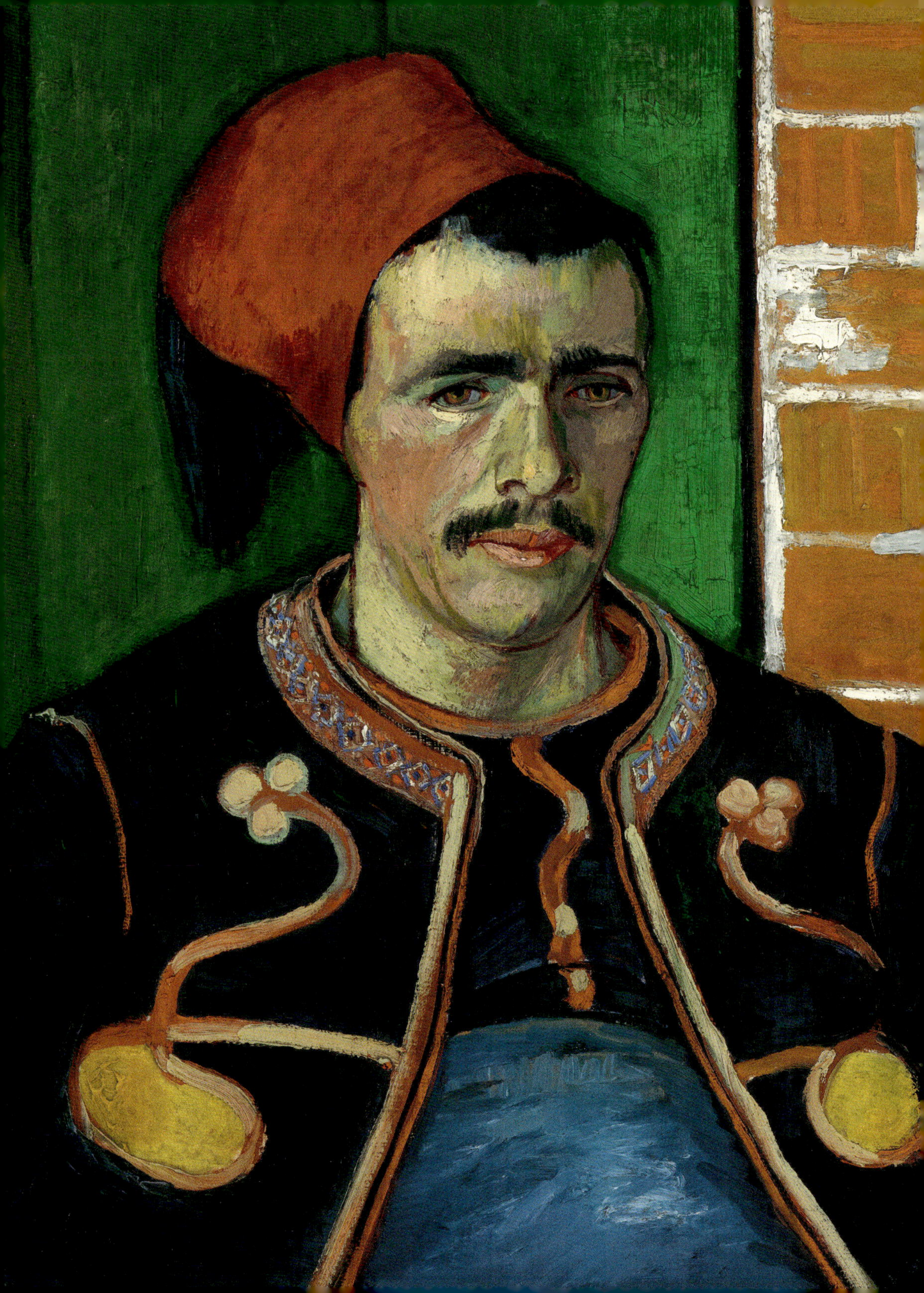

«

It is my lot, brother. Whatever you send me will never be enough. I'll always be short of money and painting supplies. I need thousands of tubes of paint and hundreds of canvases to paint what passes in front of my eyes. I painted the soldier with the tubes you sent me last week. Masses of paint went into the man. It was a fight. He looked at me from the canvas and said it wasn't good. This was missing. That was missing. This had to be this way. This had to be that way. Did he want to force my surrender? If so, he didn't know me. When I go into battle, brother, I go all the way. The struggle has to be fierce. I smeared thick slabs of colour all over his body. I scratched away his face and plastered it again. I trimmed his moustache until it fell properly. I contrasted his blackened face harshly against the pale white wall. I painted his blue uniform like a painting within a painting. Exuberant, with red and yellow decorations. I had a blue tassel fall from his blood-red cap. His orange-green tiger eyes were the hardest to capture. You can't do it, they glared. You won't grasp us, they glared. That's just what they thought. I painted them until they surrendered. I pressed the soldier's small head onto his bull neck. He let me. After the eyes his resistance was gone. It turned out quite a good portrait. The soldier was brought to his knees. Slumped on a low stool. His hands in a sign of surrender. His feet wide apart on the red stone floor. That's how the painters of that time would have painted the floor. With those baked square tiles. I want to make many more paintings like this. The way of the sunflower. As long as you continue to send me money and tubes of paint and canvas.

»

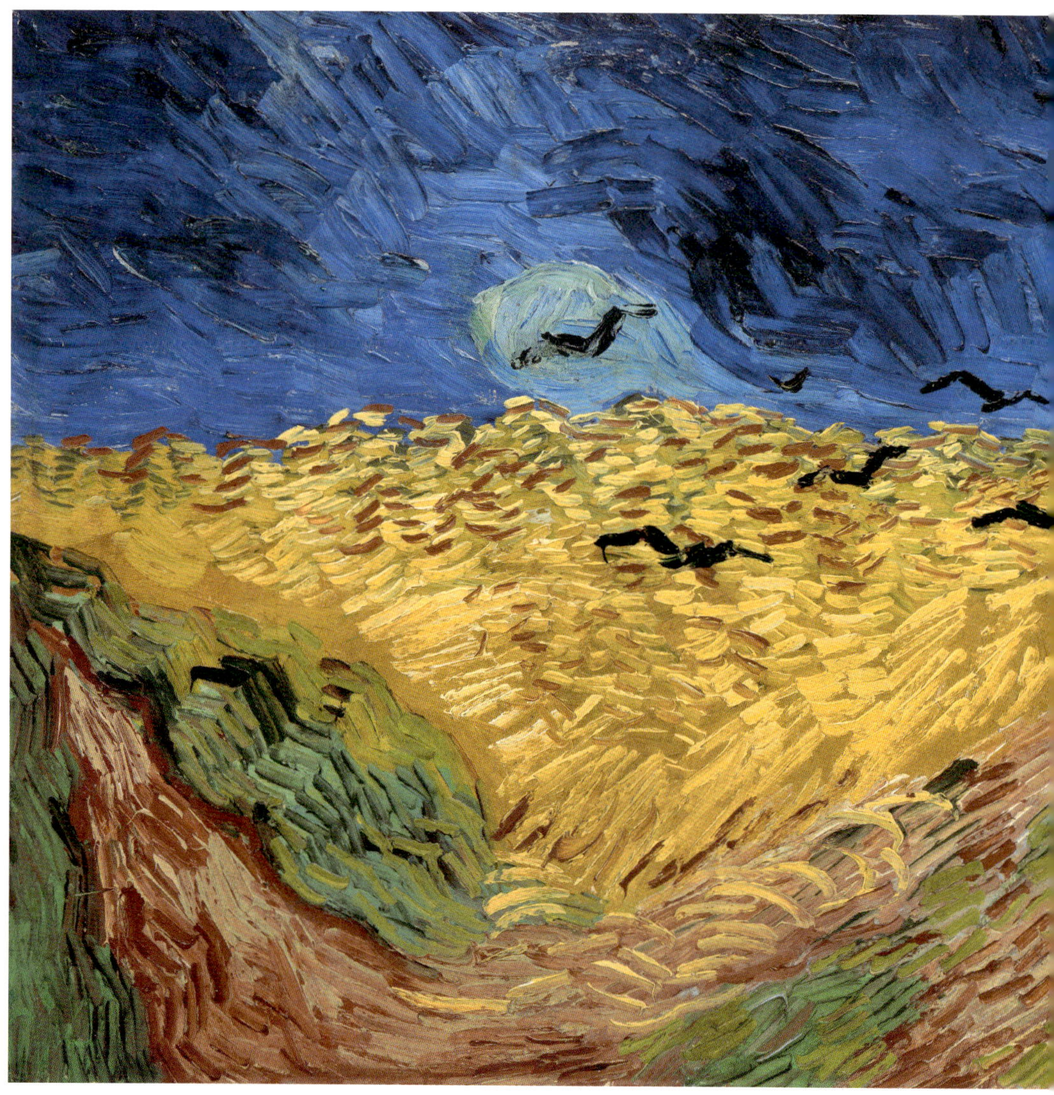

Wheatfield with Crows *1890*

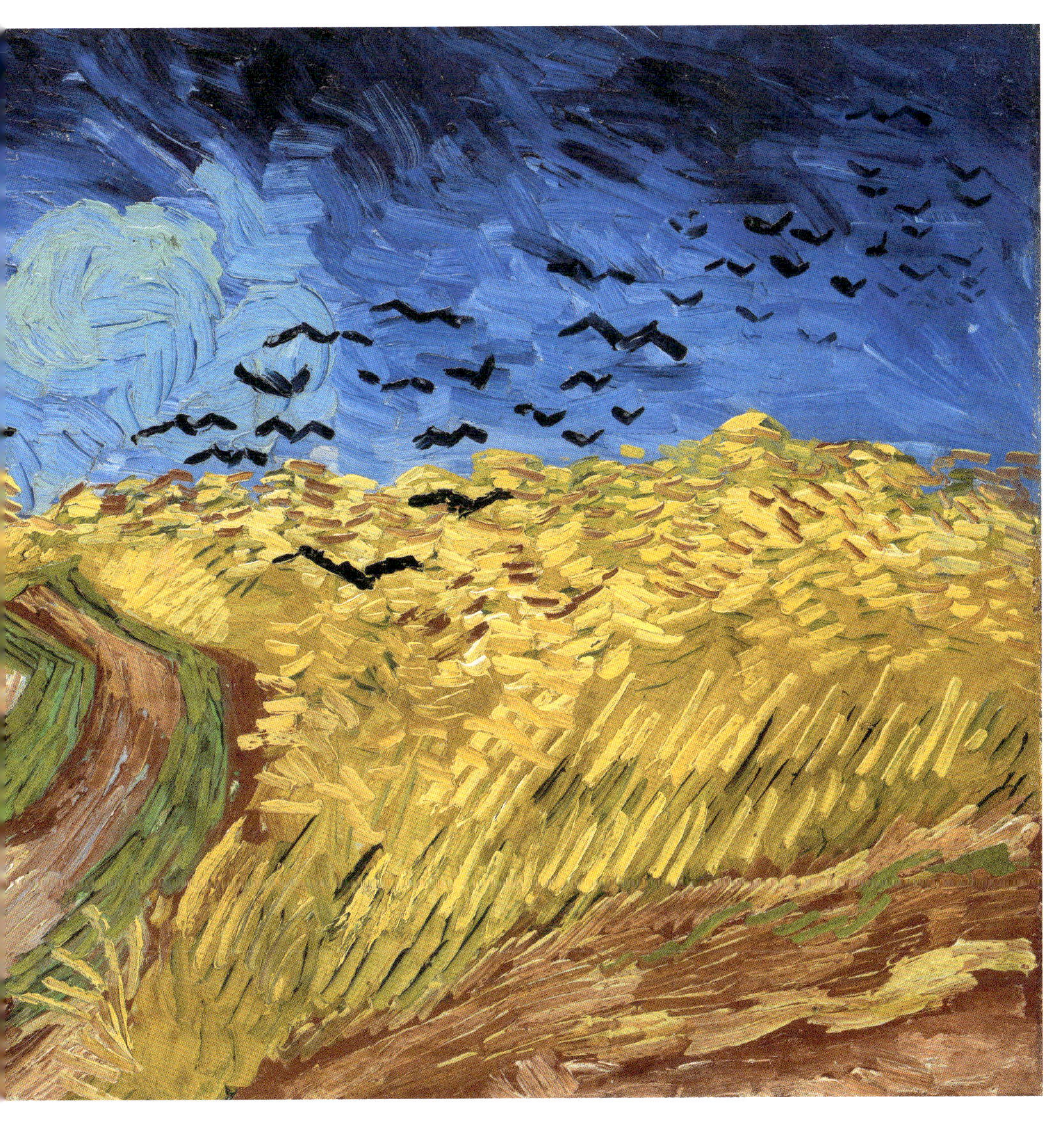

« When painting in the sun,
brother, I sing like a cricket. »

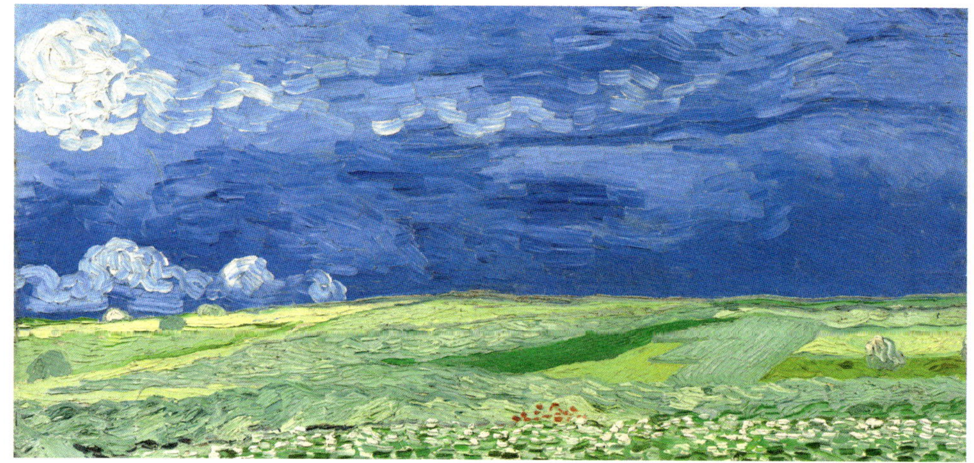

Wheatfield under Thunderclouds 1890

« I go searching for blue day and night, brother. **But slender trees I paint as black flames.** »

« There's no end to my journeying, brother. My boots are worn flat. My left big toe sticks out black and blue. I walk in the scorching sun. In a thunderstorm. Over hills. Along rivers. Through fields. A ghost in a straw hat. Sometimes I fear my straw hat will catch fire. That's how hot they bake it here. Recently I came across a sower. It was early morning. The sun was rolling over the edge of the earth like a yellow ball. We sunflowers see what people don't want to see, brother. Or what people can't see. Or what they forget to see. That the sun lights up the earth. That the sun shows us the hills. The fields. The trees. The flowers. The roofs of the houses. A treasure trove of colours. Without sun there are no colours, brother. And no shadows. Yes, shadows are colours too. Put it to the test, brother. Paint a shadow and the colours round the shadow glow brightly. The green is greener. The red redder. The blue bluer. The sower came out of the sun. I set up my easel and he stepped onto my canvas. He quickly got into his stride. His right arm swung from left to right and from right to left. It rained seeds. The earth was yellow and blue and sea blue against the sky in a sudden downpour. In a while the sun again flashed hard-as-rock yellow. In an instant the sky was on fire. I had to hurry up painting. The sower wore white trousers. Or what must once have been white trousers. Wind and weather had washed his blue coat into the most beautiful blue that can be found on earth. I painted the jacket so that the orange rattling in the blue is almost inaudible. A painter also gets what he sows, brother. Even though I don't sell a single canvas, I paint what I have to paint. The way I have to paint it.

»

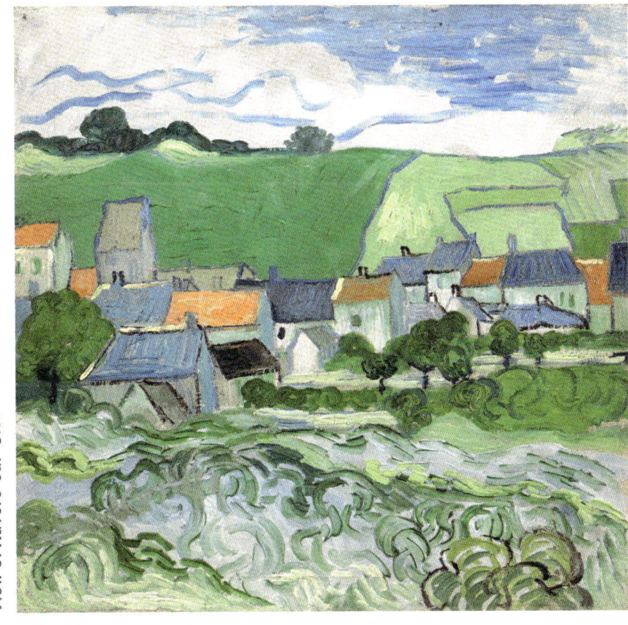

View of Auvers-sur-Oise 1890

« I end up
with the same
thing so often,
brother.
Landscape
follows portrait.
Portrait
follows
landscape. »

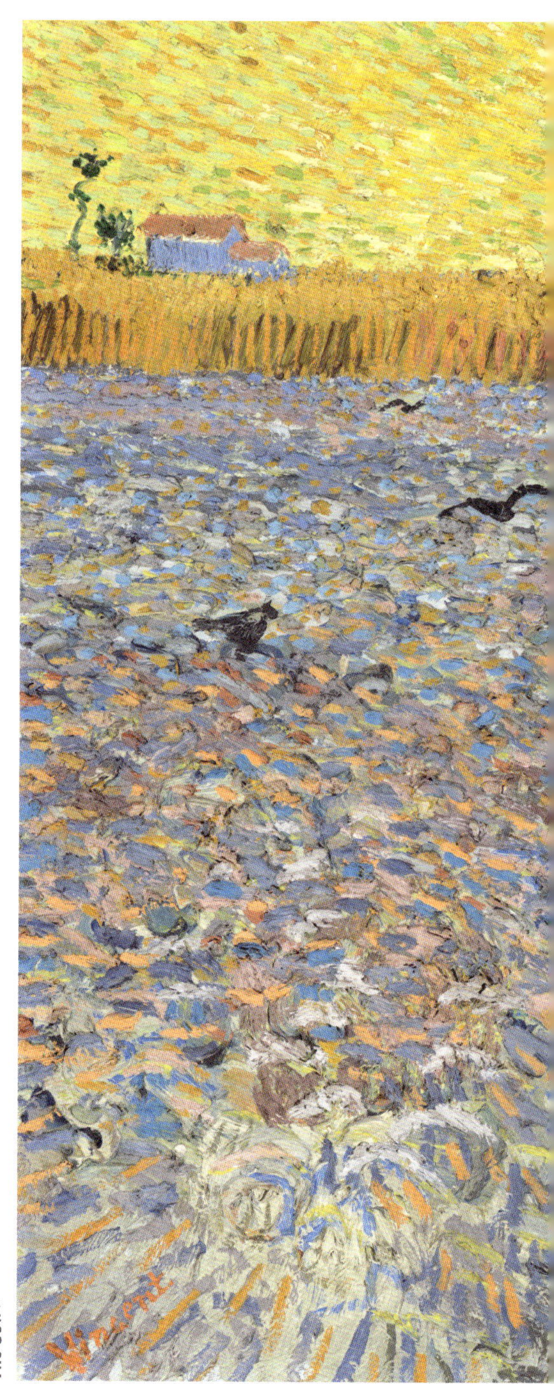

The Sower 1888

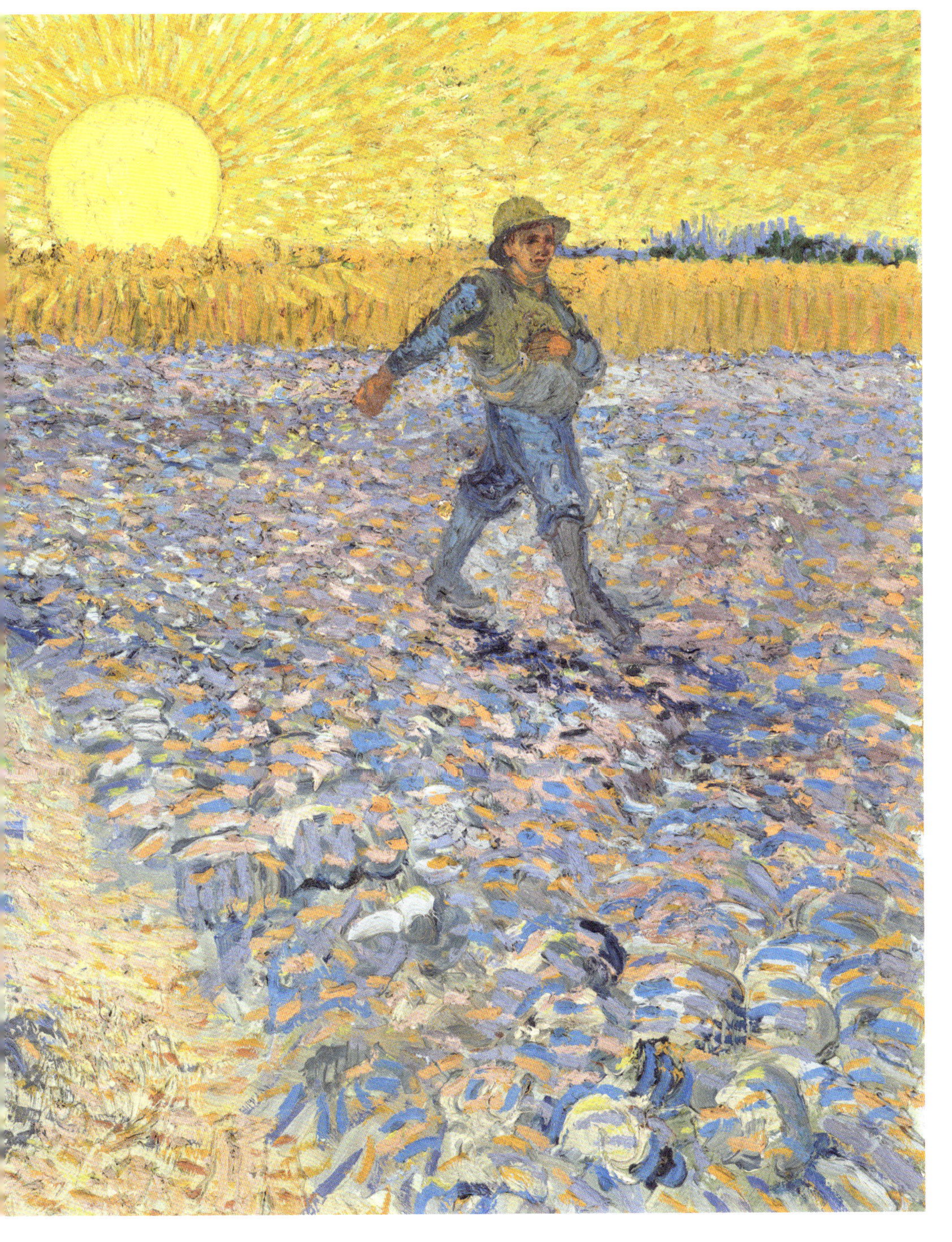

«

Faces are landscapes, brother. Made up of plains and flat areas, intersected by gorges, ravines and stubble fields. Rivers meander through them. A face-landscape bespeaks a hard or soft life. It contains pain. Joy. Poverty Heavy labour. Worry and concern. Love. Hope. Desire for happiness. Dr Paul is a gentle person, brother. I saw it immediately. Trusted him at first sight. He recognized the painter in me and I the human being in him. He saw the struggles of the painter in me. He didn't take me for a fool. He paints and draws himself. He's teaching me to etch. His face is the colour of heated brick. His hair is red, like mine. Carrot-coloured. His weird white cap covers his blue eyes. I painted him in his thick blue coat sitting at a red garden table. His blue coat makes his face and hands paler. I placed two yellow books on the table. Like sunflowers. Next to the books I placed a purple flower in a transparent glass. Dr Paul is a very good doctor, brother. He listens. He takes his time. He remains silent. He looks attentively. His sense of art is remarkable. He owns an attractive collection of drawings and paintings. The doctor has eight cats and eight dogs and chickens. Rabbits, turkeys and pigeons are also part of the family. Behind Dr Paul I painted blue hills. Not too high and rounded. Somewhat fluid. Backgrounds make a portrait, brother. They add to a portrait the environment in which the sitter exists. In a different landscape, Dr Paul would have been a different doctor. Gloomier perhaps. Hastier perhaps. Perhaps less willing to listen and remain silent. His portrait would have been a different portrait. His face would have been a different landscape.

»

Doctor Paul Gachet 1890

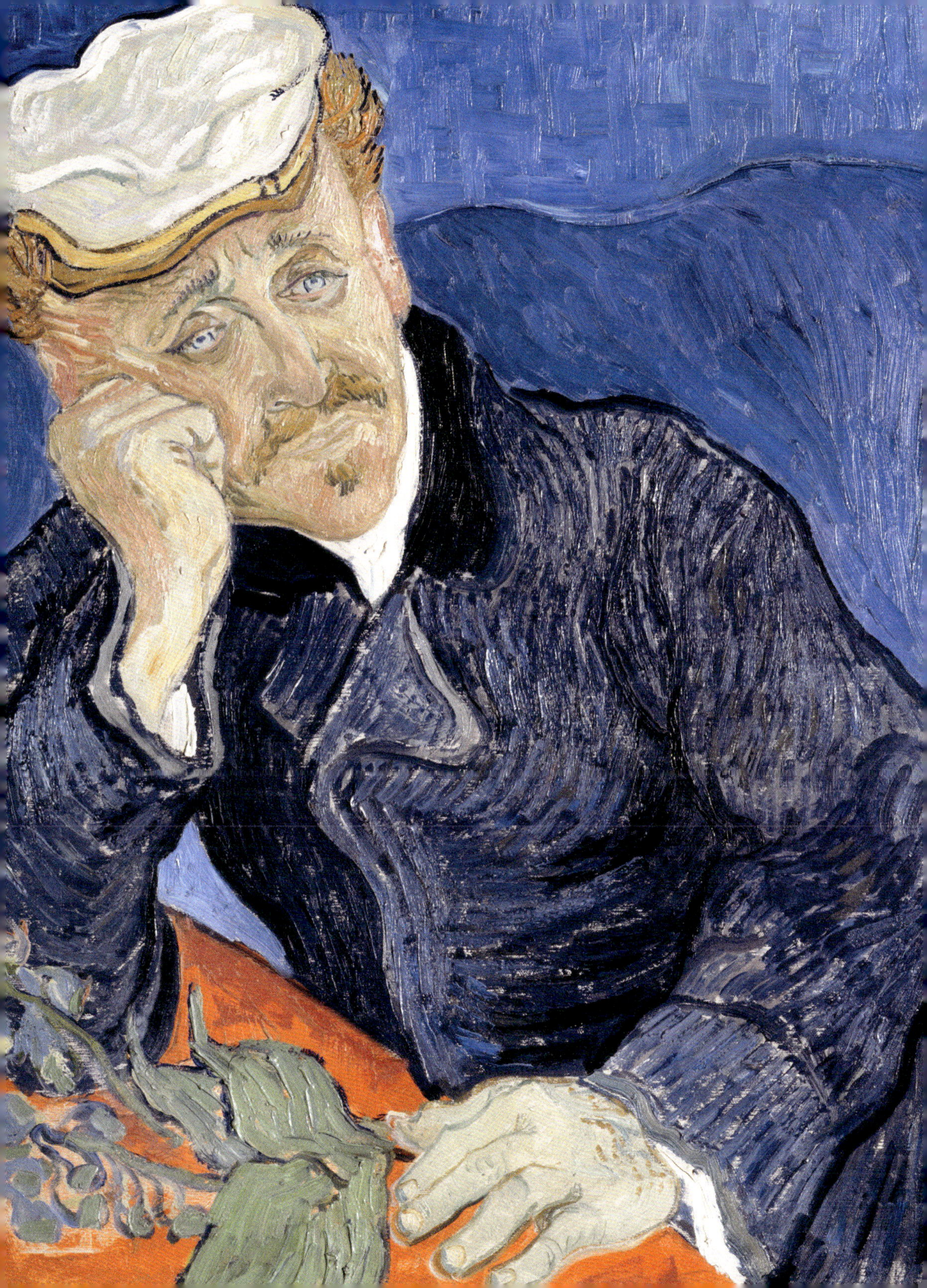

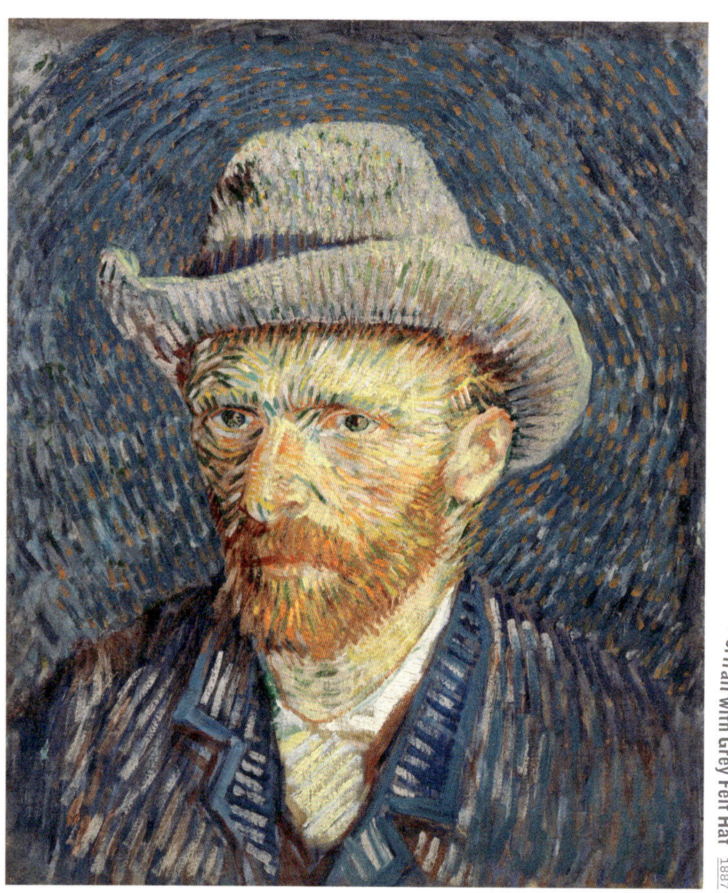

Self-Portrait with Grey Felt Hat 1887

« Bring me indoors and you'll have a big shaggy dog, brother.
One with wet paws that's always in the way and barks loudly. A dirty beast, so to speak. »

«

know some nice families, brother. They're beautiful to look at. Lots of yellow. Lots of green. The little heads turned to the sun. There's lots of laughter. But a bit too close together in my opinion. Too much locked in the same jar. Good families are oppressive. I need air. Emptiness. Fields. Forests. Mountains. Landscapes. Cornfields. I think I'm prone to cabin fever. And I'm not the nicest customer either. I can't look at the sun every hour of the day. My head hangs a little too much towards the ground. I have those days, brother. Then I walk through the landscape with my loneliness under my arm. Then I see the desolation inside me in the desolation of the landscape. Is it the world that shuts me out? Or do I shut myself out? Did I leave the house, lose the key along the way and now can't let myself back in? Take me in and I'll blossom. But a month later you'll throw me out of the door. Withered and dried out. Dr Paul's family is one of those wonderful families. It's nice. They enjoy life. There's laughter and talking. Music is played and sung. There are flowers in the house and in the garden. To make you jealous. There's a piano in the living room. Dr Paul's daughter plays excellently. When she plays, she fills the whole house with sound. She makes it rain and snow, tinkle and twinkle. She didn't want me to paint her. I begged her for a month. There was no way I wasn't going to be allowed to set her on canvas. I begged until she broke. « I'll paint you as my sister, » I promised. I kept my word. First I drew her. In the painting I stretched her. She was even more beautiful than she already was. Her eyes follow her fingers. The candle on the dark purple piano flickers. I painted the girl as she played. With many gestures. With head and body. With heart and soul. Her portrait would pair nicely with a painting of a cornfield. The piano singing in the living room, the crickets singing in the field. The singing in my canvases comes from the colour, brother. A black stripe sings a white shadow. Red and yellow sing brutally. Blue and grey calm the din. The colours all together

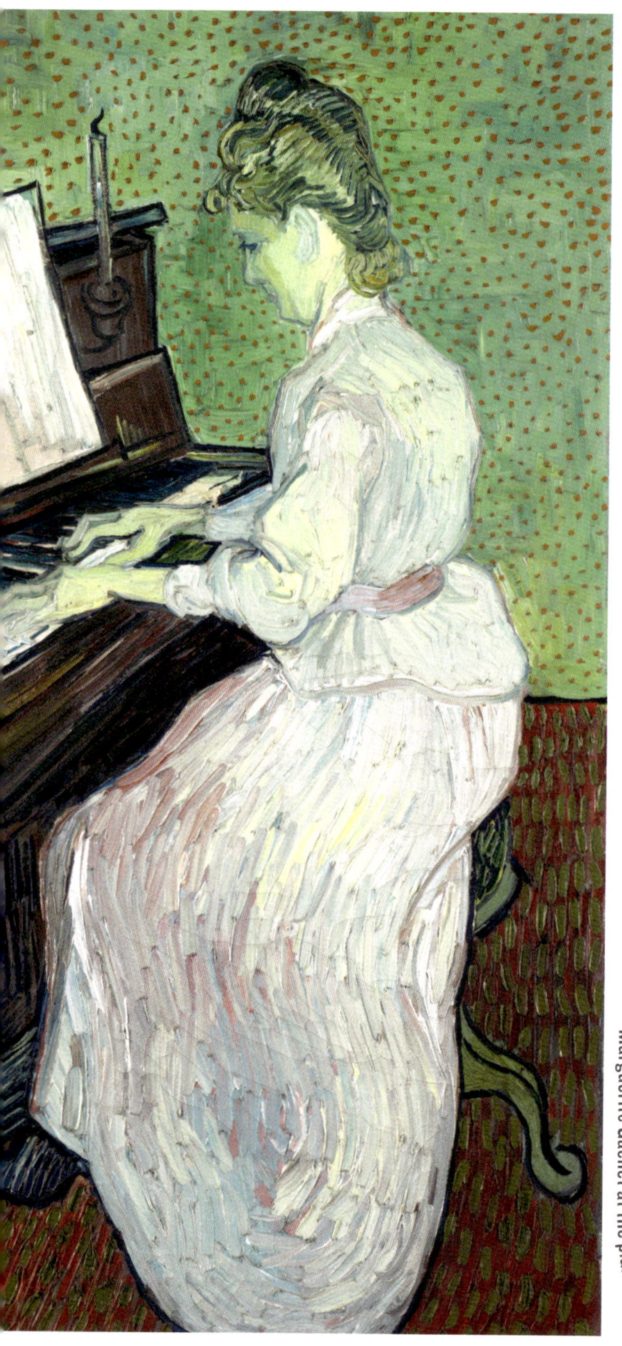

Marguerite Gachet at the piano 1890

form a choir, brother. I want to paint portraits that will still appeal to people a hundred years from now. That fill a room like a sudden apparition. With lots of expression. With a face that has a face. I want to storm heaven with quick paint-touches and small brush-flicks. You can do that only with colour. With huge amounts of colour. With heavily applied paint and with thin, rapid strokes. With full colours. With colours in the colour. Clear and bright. Colours touch the heart, brother.

»

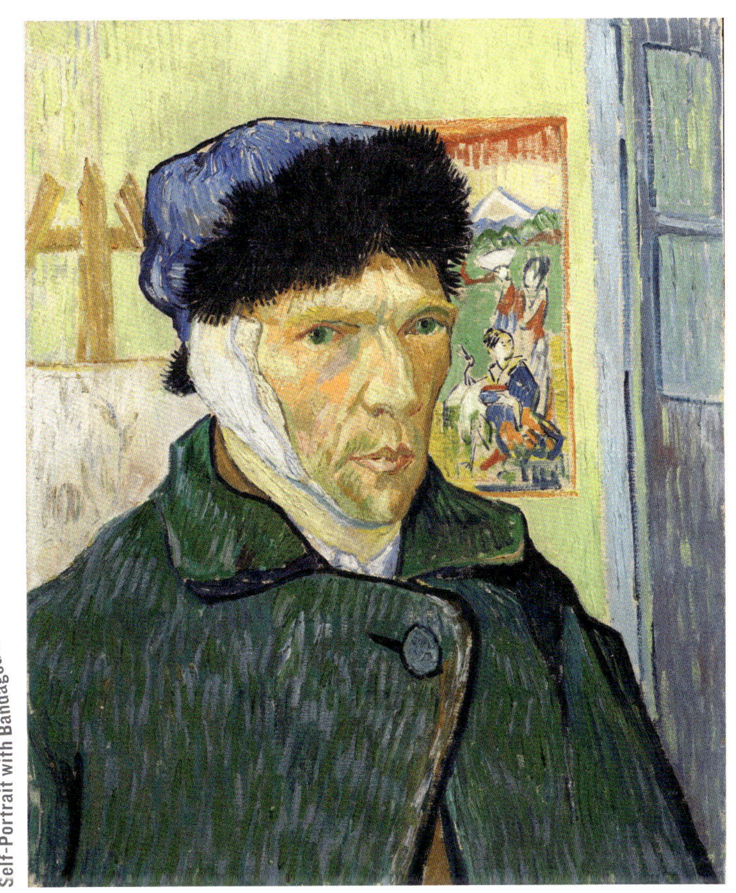

Self-Portrait with Bandaged Ear 1889

« There have to be mistakes in a painting, brother. Without mistakes a painting has no life in it. I'll cut off my ear for a good painting. »

«

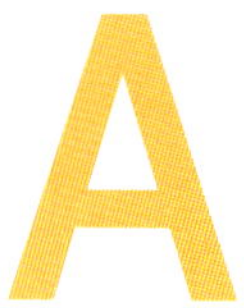

good portrait immediately speaks to the viewer, brother. It tells a story. It cannot be alone. Not hanging lonely on a wall. It wants to be seen and heard and understood. It should push the viewer around. To varying viewing angles. Close by. Face to face. Obliquely to the left. Obliquely to the right. Several steps back. Side-on. Rub your nose over a portrait and you will see streaks and smudges and strokes and sweeps of thick, oily paint and thin paint. Stand back and you'll see a person emerge from the stripes and streaks. A person with a face and a face that says something. Up close, a flat surface consists of many colours. Even if no bigger than a postage stamp, it bursts with colour. Slowly take a few steps back and you'll see all the colours merge into a single colour. Into a purple nose, a red cheek, a yellow ear, a matt face, a withered potato eater, a soldier, a sunflower. Colours scream out, brother. They trade blows. But they also caress and embrace. They soften and harden traits. They laugh. Cry. Green and red say something about pain. Yellow is a soft hand. Or a punch in the eye. Yellow can be soft as green and hard as black. And one more thing, brother. Colours erase mistakes. With mistakes in the painting, a hand that's too big, a leg that extends too far, the farmer bends out of the painting. As if he wants out of the painting. Away from the oppressive frame. Away from himself. The farmer I painted is old and poor. Doesn't he look a bit like me? Like our father? His face is perhaps coarser. I painted him in his eternal blue-green shirt, his face radiant. He has his hands around the handle of his rake. His shoulders hang loose. I smelled the farmer from afar. A smell of wild animal and hay. I also used colour to evoke his stare and smell. I wanted to breathe life into the farmer. You're right, brother. I am a painter obsessed. Obsessed with colour.

»

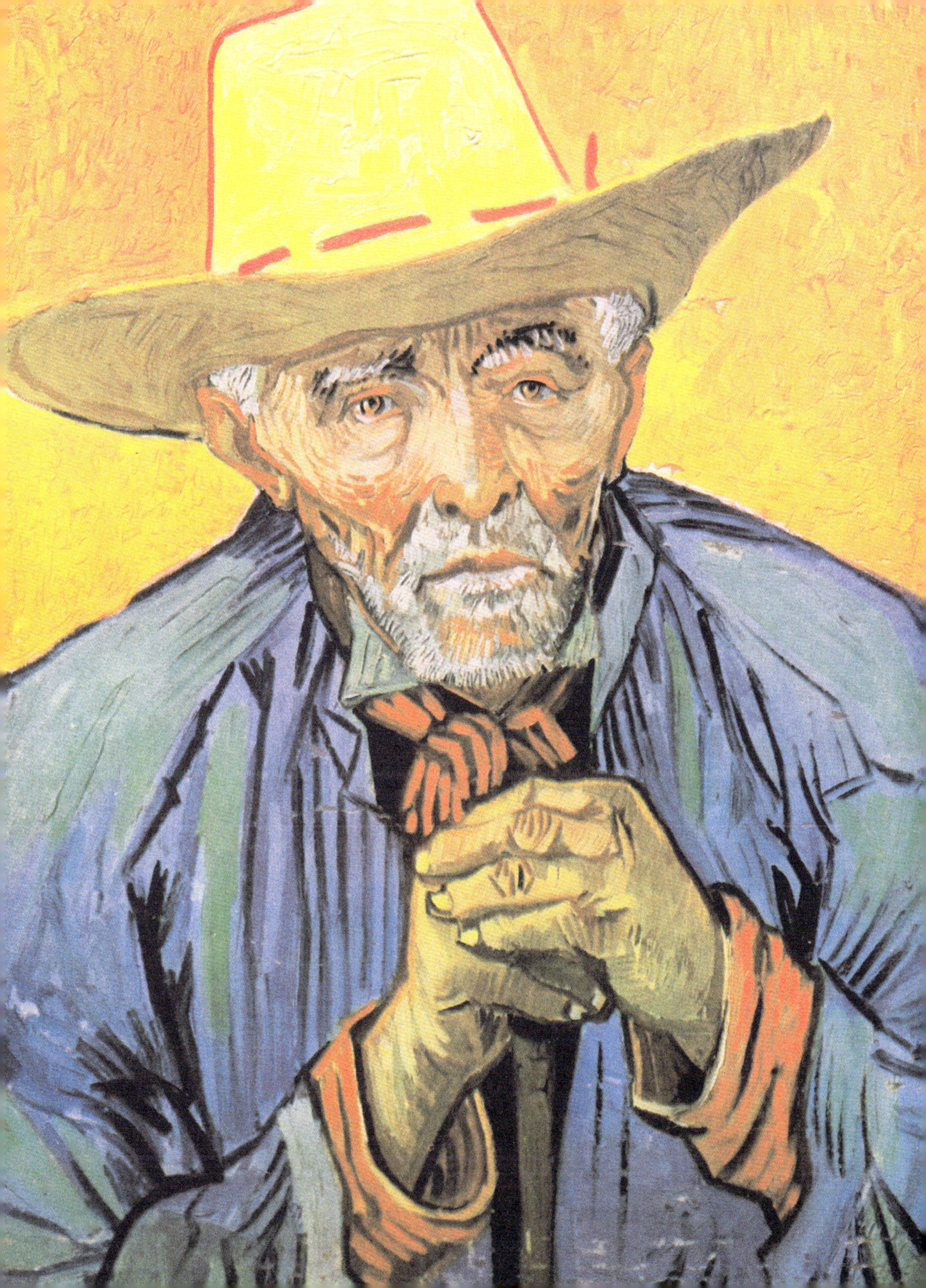

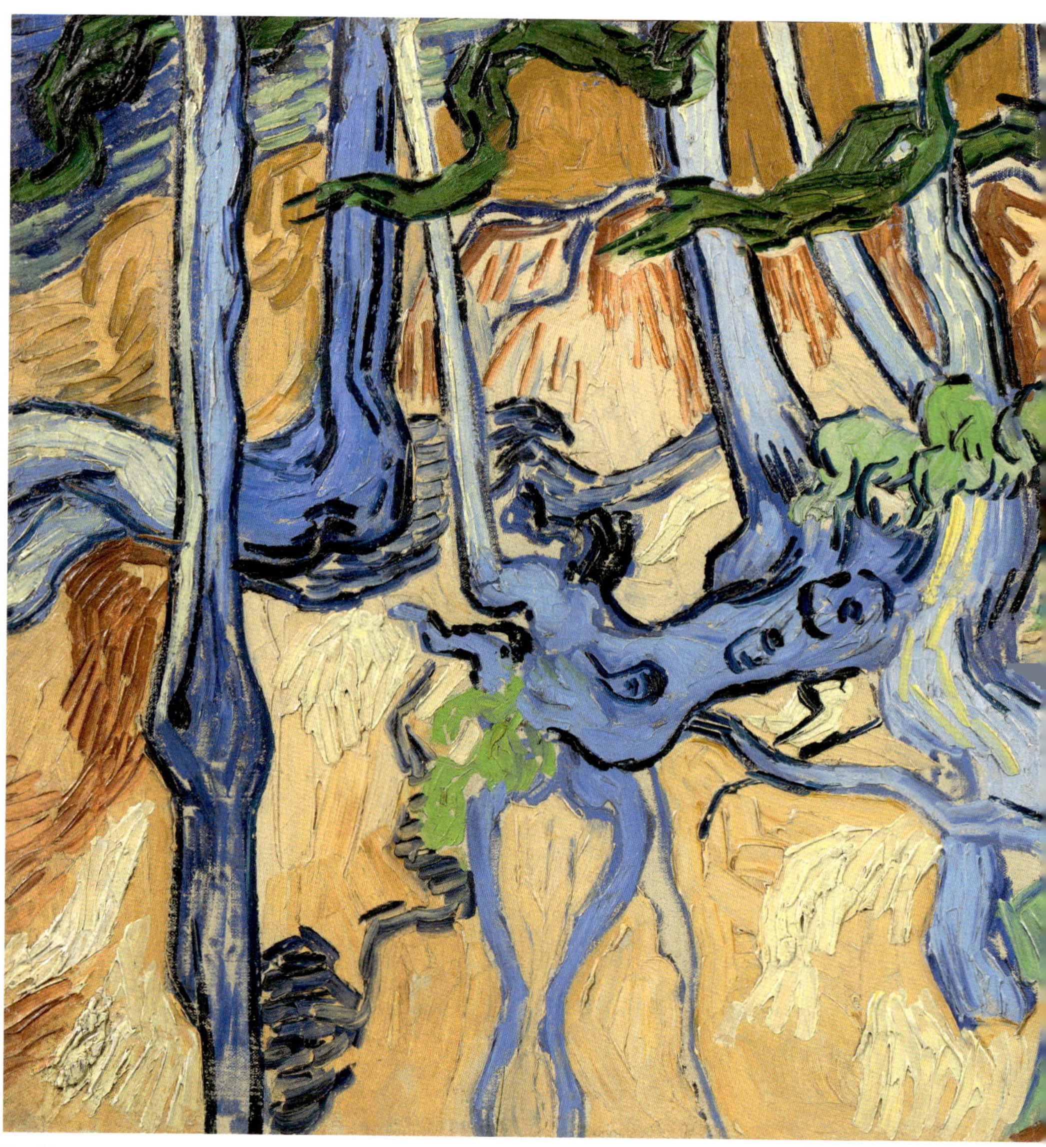

Tree Roots 1890

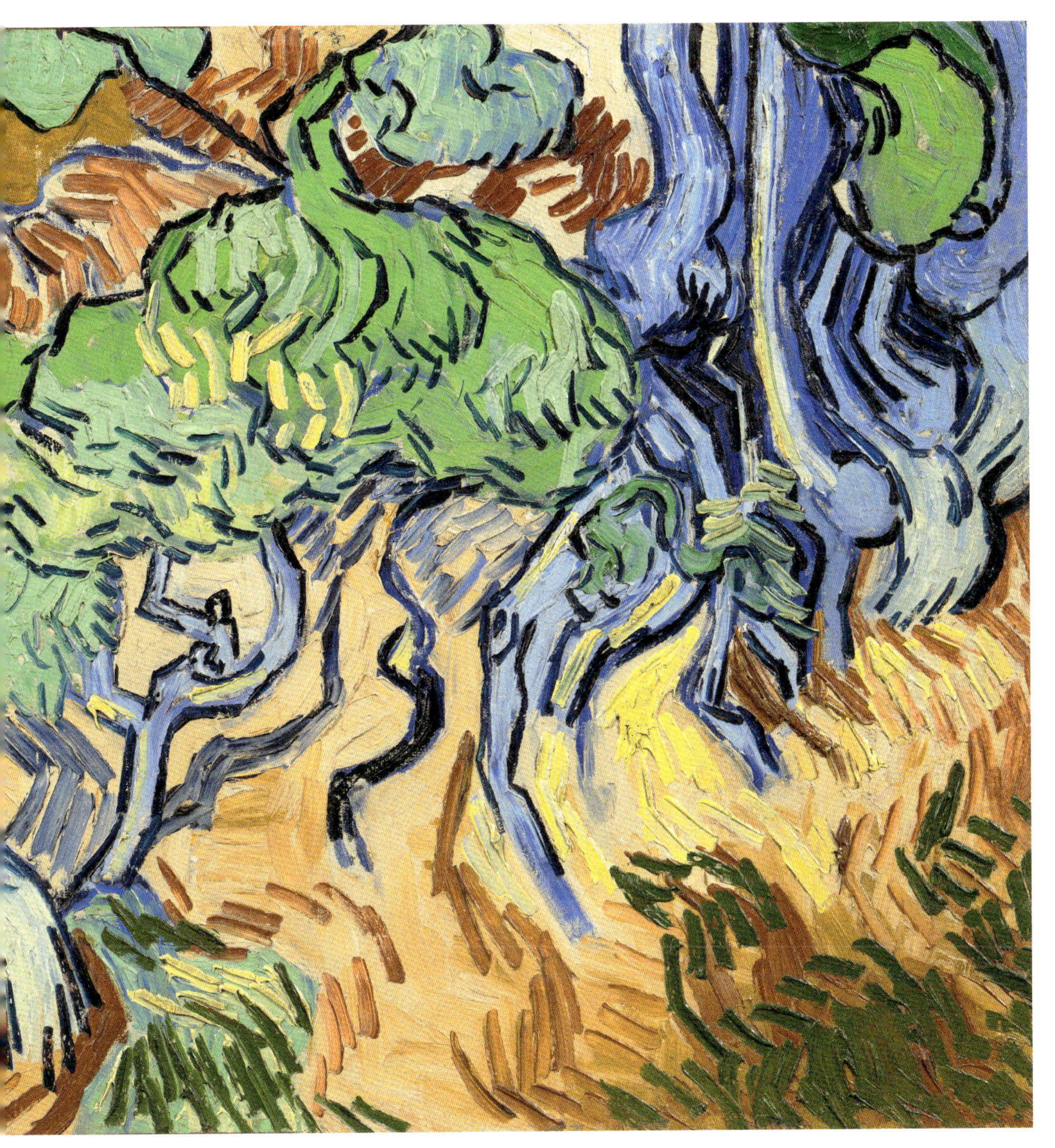

« The brushstrokes succeed each other
as if mechanically: above, through, next to,
on top of and under each other, brother.
They wind me. I need air. »

«

I am tired, brother. It's the restlessness in me. The restlessness that rages with the violence of a storm and never subsides. My head is racing. As are my heart, my eyes, my dreams. They bombard me with a hundred and one how-to questions. It's unbearable. How to paint sunflowers? How to paint fields? How to paint the chair with the candle? How to paint the sun? How to paint the teeming of the stars? How to paint the singing of a scythe? How to paint the suffering of worn-out shoes? How to paint green? How to paint blue? How to portray myself in my paintings? The closer I get to grasping an image, the further it recedes from me. A hill approaches and disappears. A face approaches and fades away. A blooming flower loses its leaves. As if I wanted to step on my shadow. As if I wanted to figure out the point at which I fall asleep. I know and I don't know. I can and I can't. Just before I grasp the leaf from the tree, the wind blows it away. I'm running my heart out. I grab and I catch and I catch air. It's enough to make me tear my hair out. To make me... I painted the wicker chair with short green and red strokes. To place it on canvas as it is. Dark brown-red with bluish shadows. The seat green and straw yellow. Next to the burning candle a yellowish, pinkish book. I didn't finish the book. No time. No courage. Too restless. The gas lamp is a spinning star. I painted the chair until the room was empty and deserted. No sunflowers on the wall. The front leg of the chair is also saying it wants to leave the room, that it too wants to exit the painting. With a final brushstroke I closed the door behind me. Maybe someday someone will pick up the book from the chair, brother. Maybe someday someone will read it to the end for me. Who knows. Kisses.

»

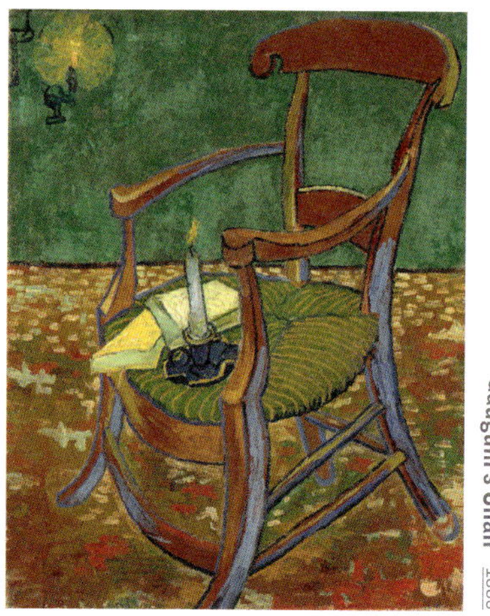

Gauguin's Chair 1888

List of illustrations

31 **Shoes, Paris, September-November 1886**
Oil on canvas, 38.1 × 45.3 cm
Van Gogh Museum, Amsterdam
(Vincent van Gogh Foundation)

33 **Postman Joseph Roulin, 1888**
Oil on canvas, 81.3 × 65.4 cm
Museum of Fine Arts, Boston,
Gift of Robert Treat Paine
Photo: © Scala, Florence

34 **Self-Portrait, 1889**
Oil on canvas, 51.5 × 45 cm
Nasjonalmuseet, Oslo
Photo: © Børre Høstland

35 **La Mousmé, 1888**
Oil on canvas, 73.3 × 60.3 cm
Chester Dale Collection, National Gallery of Art, Washington

36 **The Zouave, Arles, June 1888**
Oil on canvas, 65.8 cm × 55.7 cm
Van Gogh Museum, Amsterdam
(Vincent van Gogh Foundation)

38 **Wheatfield with Crows, Auvers-sur-Oise, July 1890**
Oil on canvas, 50.5 × 103 cm
Van Gogh Museum, Amsterdam
(Vincent van Gogh Foundation)

40 **Wheatfield under Thunderclouds, Auvers-sur-Oise, July 1890**
Oil on canvas, 50.4 × 101.3 cm
Van Gogh Museum, Amsterdam
(Vincent van Gogh Foundation)

41 **View of Auvers-sur-Oise, Auvers-sur-Oise, May-June 1890**
Oil on canvas, 50.2 × 52.5 cm
Van Gogh Museum, Amsterdam
(Vincent van Gogh Foundation)

42 **The Sower, c. 17–28 June 1888**
Oil on canvas, 64.2 × 80.3 cm
Kröller-Müller Museum, Otterlo

45 **Doctor Paul Gachet, 1890**
Oil on canvas, 68.2 × 57 cm
Musée d'Orsay, Parijs
Photo: © RMN-Grand Palais
(musée d'Orsay)/Gérard Blot

46 **Self-Portrait with Grey Felt Hat, Paris, September-October**
Oil on canvas, 44.5 × 37.2 cm
Van Gogh Museum, Amsterdam
(Vincent van Gogh Foundation)

48 **Marguerite Gachet at the Piano, 26–27 June 1890**
Oil on canvas, 102.5 × 50 cm
Kunstmuseum Basel

49 **Self-Portrait with Bandaged Ear, January 1889**
Oil on canvas, 60 × 49 cm
The Courtauld Institute, London
Photo: © The Courtauld/
Bridgeman Images

51 **Portrait of Patience Escalier, Arles, 1888**
Oil on canvas, 69 × 56 cm
Collection Stavros S. Niarchos

52 **Tree Roots, Auvers-sur-Oise, July 1890**
Oil on canvas, 50.3 × 100.1 cm
Van Gogh Museum, Amsterdam
(Vincent van Gogh Foundation)

54 **Gauguin's Chair, Arles, November 1888**
Oil on canvas, 90.5 × 72.7 cm
Van Gogh Museum, Amsterdam
(Vincent van Gogh Foundation)

For Nona

Many thanks to Hilde Van der Sypt, Marc Verstraeten, Karin Borghouts, Sandra Zographos, Steve & Ruth Curson and to everyone (and every institution) who contributed enthusiastically to this book. Thank you.

— Paul de Moor

This is a publication of Snoeck Publishers, Sint-Kwintensberg 83, 9000 Ghent
Director Philip Van Bost
Publisher Gunther De Wit

Author Paul de Moor
Proofreading Sue Pickles
Translation Michael Lomax
Graphic Design Thijs Kestens, Armée de Verre Bookdesign

ISBN 9789461618931
D/2024/0012/10

www.snoeckpublishers.be

Published with the support of

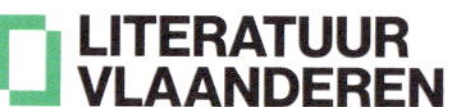